Praise for *The Boys*

"Katie Hafner's taut and utterly delightful debut is a novel of multitudes. It is travel escapism, a family drama, a character study, social commentary on pandemic isolation and an incredible journey back to center. We are emerging from a period of forced introversion, and *The Boys* provides the perfect antidote. . . ."

—Weike Wang, *New York Times Book Review*

"*The Boys* is a treat with a surprise inside. Readers will undoubtedly agree."

—*Publishers Weekly*

"Tender and emotionally intelligent. . . . An audacious feat of narrative bravado."

—Maria Semple, *New York Times* bestselling
author of *Where'd You Go, Bernadette*

"A brilliant, thoughtful novel that comes with perhaps the greatest shocker in recent literature (no spoiler alert). A superb meditation on loneliness and community."

—Gary Shteyngart, *New York Times* bestselling
author of *Our Country Friends*

"*The Boys* is utterly charming—one of the most delightful books I have read in ages. As we bike through Italy's little villages with introvert Ethan Fawcett, stopping to drink a *caffè shakerato* as church bells ring in a mournful E flat, what we see around us is the wide and beautiful horizon of the human heart. I absolutely loved this little miracle of a book."

—Meg Waite Clayton, *New York Times* bestselling
author of *The Postmistress of Paris*

"This is a treat-yourself read, the tale of an endearing human on a hilariously misguided quest for love and connection, in the delight-filled tradition of Anne Tyler. But Hafner bakes a surprise into the center of her confection—a glorious, mind-blowing twist that propels the story to unexpected heights and depths. With exquisite compassion and humor, this novel leaves its readers deeply nourished, heart, mind, and soul."

—Debra Jo Immergut, author of *You Again* and *The Captives*

"Unexpectedly funny, touching, disarming—*The Boys* got under my skin from the very first page. Hafner is a wry and wise explorer of the secrets buried deep in our most intimate relationships. This novel will stay with me for a long time."

—Laura Zigman, author of *Separation Anxiety*

The
Boys

Katie Hafner

Spiegel
and Grau

Spiegel & Grau, New York
www.spiegelandgrau.com

Copyright © 2022 by Katie Hafner

Jacket design by Strick&Williams
Interior design by Meighan Cavanaugh

Cover illustration by Manshen Lo

Library of Congress Cataloging-in-Publication Data Available Upon Request

ISBN 978-1-954118-34-8 (TP)
ISBN 978-1-954118-06-5 (eBook)

Printed in the United States of America on
30 percent postconsumer recycled paper

First Hardback Edition 2022
First Paperback Edition 2023
10 9 8 7 6 5 4 3 2 1

For Zoë, my inspiration for this story . . .

and so much more.

The Boys

Prologue

Mr. Ethan Fawcett
225 St. Marks Square
Philadelphia, PA 19104

10 August 2022

Dear Mr. Fawcett,

Thank you for joining Hill and Dale Adventures on our recent journey through Piedmont, Italy. At Hill and Dale we strive to accommodate our guests fully, and we pride ourselves in giving all Hill and Dalers peace of mind in order to enjoy the special joys of active travel. We consider our planning and support unparalleled.

However, in our 27 years of operation, we have not encountered a guest with requirements as unique as yours. Unfortunately, your unusual circumstances made it difficult for us to meet your needs, and those of your two boys. After careful consideration, we have concluded that Hill and Dale is not a good fit for your particular set of needs, and we have decided it would be best for you not to return for future excursions with our company.

All the very best to you.

Sincerely,

Roger Hill

Roger Hill
President & CEO, Hill and Dale Adventures

Part One

Ethan and Barb

1.

I WAS STANDING IN THE FRONT HALLWAY SORTING THROUGH a stack of mail and didn't notice Barb on the other side of the screen door. Then came her little taps on the doorframe, the same cadence I'd heard hundreds of times at the dinner table. It was her *you're-beginning-to-bore-me-to-death* signal. The telltale pattern of Barb's long beautiful fingers was a single tap followed by three staccatos, then repeated half a dozen times—taaap tap tap tap. Irritating. But effective.

As soon as I turned my head in her general direction, Barb opened the door and stepped inside. In one hand she was holding a large Ziploc bag filled with cookies. In the other she held a piece of paper. At the sight of the paper in her hand, I felt my palms grow clammy.

"This came to my email by mistake," she said. "I printed it out for you." I was instantly relieved that she hadn't come to present divorce papers. But I was also bewildered. Why had she bothered to print out and hand-deliver whatever this was? Then I recognized the unmistakable Hill and Dale logo.

Barb was talking while I read. "What did you do, Ethan? You went on the same trip? Why didn't you tell me you were going? And you took the boys? To Italy? What were you thinking? And you hate traveling!"

I was still absorbing the contents of the letter. Unusual circumstances? Peace of mind? Whose peace of mind were they referring to?

"Ethan? Are you going to say anything to me?"

"I thought things went pretty well," I said meekly.

I couldn't bring myself to raise my head from the page I held and look at Barb. She forced the issue by waving the bag of cookies at me. She was looking straight at me, her mouth set in a perfect horizontal line. "They're chocolate chip," she announced solemnly. She pressed the Ziploc into my hand.

I held the bag up to the light to examine the cookies. Walnuts. Really? Could she be more clueless?

The boys' health issues—particularly their food allergies—had never been much of a priority for Barb. Plus, she thought the whole allergy business was overblown. "You know," she'd say, while I did laps around the living room with the vacuum, "research is starting to show that kids exposed to dirt and dust have lower rates of asthma when they're older." That was only one of our many little disagreements. They seemed small enough in isolation, though their cumulative effect led to relational drag, like ice accumulating on the wings of an airplane. Later she stopped commenting on this and that foible and started obsessing about the "large torn canvas" of our marriage. I pressed the Ziploc, checking for air leaks.

"I don't know what to say." Her thick hair was pulled back, but I could tell she'd cut it, maybe even to shoulder length. Her clothes sagged on her. She looked like she'd lost weight. She let out a sigh that told me there was a lot more she wanted to say but was choosing not to.

"I just can't believe you took the boys. To Italy?" Her hushed tone heightened the impact. I'd have preferred a scream.

Still, the effect was the same. Her 105 pounds had transformed into a menacing hulk. She lifted her eyes toward the ceiling, then leveled them at me again. "If going on the bike trip was something you really wanted to do, they could have stayed with me."

My head swam with half a dozen possible comebacks to that one: *Barb, you were away at one of your conferences.* (This was true). Or: *You mean you didn't know I had it in me to take them on an adventure like that? Well, surprise surprise!* Or maybe this: *Give them to you only to expose them to hazards like this?* I held up the cookies in a hapless pantomime, which of course was lost on her.

Instead, my reply was so feeble I felt humiliated even before I opened my mouth to speak.

"Really, Barb, what am I supposed to do?" My throat closed down around the last couple of words, and when they emerged, I sounded like I was testing an oboe reed.

She was quiet again. "Where are they?"

"In their room," I said. "I think they're taking a nap. We're all still jet-lagged. I can go check."

"No, that's okay. I really came to see how you are." Then she touched my arm for an instant. Her touch was so light it just brushed the hair without making contact with my skin. A familiar tingle of desire I had long since tamped down found its way in pinpoint form to the very spot she had touched.

She was wearing her concerned look. "Ethan, you need some help. Real help."

Now I was annoyed. "Barb, thanks for the cookies, which, as-you-may-recall, the boys can't eat. I need to make dinner."

"Please eat the cookies, Ethan. You're too thin." She paused, searching for what to say next. Then she added softly, as if by way of conciliation, "Eat them even if the boys can't. I baked them for you." She turned and left. I watched as she folded herself into the old red Yaris with the dent down the driver's side—*our* old red Yaris—and backed out of the driveway. I looked at the bag of cookies, still in my right hand, and then at the letter from Hill and Dale in my left. I had to wonder if she was right. Maybe I shouldn't have taken the boys. No. She was wrong. Of course I should have taken the boys. For starters, they were my children, and I was their primary custodian. It was up to me to decide what was or wasn't in their best interest. Besides, it was when I was with them that I felt most alive.

2.

IT'S A GOOD THING BARB ARRIVED WHEN SHE DID, BECAUSE I definitely didn't want her around when I started making dinner for Tommy and Sam. When she pulls one of her drop-bys and catches me fussing over the boys, I can't decipher what she's thinking. The look on her face (is it pain? embarrassment?) is a distraction I can do without, and things grow awkward quickly. I detect judgment coming from her, which I chalk up to her disdain for my insistence on routine. She used to find it endearing.

Routine is critical, especially when it comes to cooking dinner for Tommy and Sam, picky eaters who have trouble gaining weight. Add to that their allergies, and total focus and planning are required. The complicated dinner routine was another area where Barb and I diverged during our time together. Barb is spontaneous. I'm a planner. Take this Hill and Dale trip, for example. I bought the plane tickets early enough to snag an entire row for the boys and me. Barb would have procrastinated about the flight until it was too late for such ideal seating. Then, when we ended up in seats miles from each other, she would have said, "Oh well. We'll just have to make the best of it."

Thinking back on the planning for the flight made me replay the entire trip, and that made me wonder how things could have gone differently. Izzy was definitely the saving grace. If it hadn't been for her quick thinking, we wouldn't have found easy shelter from the rain that day, and we'd never have stumbled on that choir practice in the church. Still, it's not Izzy but Barb I have to thank for the outsized role that Hill and Dale came to play in my life.

Standing in the hallway with the bag of nut-laden cookies still in my hand, I suddenly felt too exhausted to go through the whole convoluted exercise of preparing dinner. Besides, the boys were still napping, hardly clamoring for a meal. Just this once, I thought, we could skip dinner. I opened the Ziploc and retrieved a cookie. I had to admit it was delicious, with the perfect amount of crunch on the perimeter, a soft center, and chocolate so dark and rich it was almost tangy. I reached into the bag for another.

. . . .

Barb and I first met when she was still in grad school and we were both working at Rita Receptionists, an answering service started in 2010 in response to people's growing frustration with voice mail. The company's operating philosophy was simple: *Phones Should Be Answered by Humans*. Companies around the country hired us to answer their phones from Philadelphia, and we did our level best to create the illusion that an actual receptionist was sitting in Seattle or Moab or San Diego. I was hired in 2010 as the first official employee. I'd met the two Rita founders in college, when I was a senior and they were getting their MBAs at Wharton, where I worked part-time doing IT support. When they started Rita, they got in touch with me and said they needed a computer wizard to write all the software from scratch. They made me chief technology officer.

Rita receptionists were trained to give the impression that they worked for the company being called. That seemed like a lot to ask of people who were being paid just a little over minimum wage, sitting in a soulless office building on Chestnut Street in West Philadelphia. Rita's founders talked a lot about "delivering an outstanding customer experience." At the time, that sounded to me like a bunch of marketing mumbo jumbo. But if you stop to think about how automated and alienating the entire service economy has become, those two guys were prophets.

Rita Receptionists (the name was a nod to a Beatles song the founders liked) took off quickly, and by the time I met Barb, my stock options looked like they might actually be worth something. Barb was getting her PhD in psychology at Penn, and she started working at Rita part-time one summer, on the 5:00 p.m.–to–9:00 p.m. extended-hours shift. I often worked late, so I saw her a lot. She usually wore a thin pale-blue cardigan, which she would drape across the back of her chair. I guessed that the sweater had been in her life for a good long time. For some reason, the sight of the cardigan on the back of that cheesy Office Depot chair struck me as regal. Within a few days of her starting at Rita, I began with some regularity to look for the chair with the cardigan. After a month, if I spotted the chair unoccupied but the sweater still there, a quiet joy came over me.

Barb's was a subtle beauty. At five foot four, she wasn't that much shorter than me, but there was a lightness to her that made her seem smaller. She wore no makeup—at least not to work—and kept her thick strawberry blond hair swept back into a barrette. I fantasized more than once about what all that hair would look like without the barrette, the loosed sheaf cascading across her back.

One evening, I approached her desk on the pretext of needing to switch out a set of cables on her computer. I had vowed that morning to ask her out. She was on a call. I lurked around her cubicle waiting for her to finish, while also eavesdropping. The extended-hours calls usually came in from the West Coast, but sometimes they were from people just looking for someone to talk to. I guessed that Barb was dealing with one of those. She was nodding, as if the caller could see her. Unlike a lot of the receptionists at Rita, she stayed focused on the conversation: "I'm so sorry about that," she was saying, while absentmindedly pulling pills from a sleeve of her sweater. She placed each tiny knot of wool on a growing pile of pills next to her keyboard. "The office is closed, but I can get a message to customer service for you. . . . Oh, I agree with you about batteries. Every time you turn around, another battery has to be replaced. . . . No, I don't own one myself, but it does sound like a handy thing to have around the house." She made conversing sound so easy. Hearing her on that call blew my heart wide open.

After she hung up, I switched out the cable quickly, hoping she wouldn't notice how unnecessary that was. I stole a closer look at all the sweater pills clustered on top of each other. It took everything I had to open my mouth. To give you a sense of how unusual such a move was for me, let me just say this: I possess more than my share of aversions, and speaking to people I hardly know is one of them. I had a sudden flash of something I could have sworn my mother once said as she practically pushed me onto the school bus, a thing I dreaded daily: "Have heart, Ethan sweetie. Another word for heart is *coeur*, and that's where we get our word *courage*." Now my heart was racing, each beat a small thunderclap in my chest. But before I knew it, I had asked Barb if she'd like to get a cup of coffee and a slice of pie at the all-night diner across the street, Miss Flo's. As the words left my mouth, this suddenly felt like a very 1950s thing to suggest, but also somehow fitting. Barb looked straight at me with those wide-set green eyes. She had a slightly startled look on her face. She told me a few months later that she and a couple of other Rita receptionists had wondered if I had a speech impediment of some kind, because they had never heard me speak.

Her look of surprise quickly softened into a gentle smile. "Sure! That sounds great," she said.

Predictably enough, things at the diner started off awkwardly. Barb headed for one of the front booths, but I stopped her and stammered my way through something about not sitting under the AC because she had just the thin sweater, and the draft under the vent could be brutal. She seemed to appreciate that, and we took a booth near the back. Barb loved the tabletop jukebox. It was a Seeburg Wall-O-Matic, beckoning from its square, neon-lit chrome box. It took dimes.

She flipped through the selections wide-eyed, murmuring that she had never seen such a thing. She chose Aretha Franklin singing "Respect." Even after the song started, Barb kept flipping through the selections. I could tell that she was enjoying the tactile encounter with the stiff tabs.

"I can't believe I've been at Rita for months and I've never come here," she said.

I didn't want Barb to know that I was all too familiar with Miss Flo's, that the wait staff knew first the two Rita cofounders and me as the three guys who came in with their laptops and stayed for hours, and then just me, the nerd, still with his laptop, but always alone, now that the two business-school guys were both busy with girlfriends and the growing company. When Barb picked up her menu, I had to stop myself from recommending the chocolate cream pie. I didn't want to come off as a know-it-all. When the waitress arrived at our table, if she was surprised to see I had company or that my computer was missing, she didn't show it.

Barb was frowning while she studied the menu. She looked up, not at the waitress but at me. "Sometimes I get decision paralysis when it comes to ordering," she said. "I don't want to be disappointed."

"Pretend it's a song in the jukebox?" I suggested. "Even if you aren't happy with your choice, you get a chance at something different next time."

"Hmm," she said, and turned back to the menu. "Maybe." She said the *maybe* slowly, quietly appraising my idea and thus me.

The waitress gave up on Barb and looked at me. I ordered the chocolate cream pie. Barb finally ordered the apple pie, heated and à la mode. I hated myself for not jumping in. Of all the pies, that was probably the worst possible choice. Gooey canned apple filling and too much cinnamon. Sure enough, as soon as her slice arrived—a viscous ooze between layers of soggy crust—I could tell she was privately miserable.

I slid my plate to the middle of the table and she did the same with hers. No words required.

Barb went back to choosing songs. "Thriller." "Tuxedo Junction." "The Twist." We had only six dimes between us, so she got up, went over to the cashier, and returned with a pile of them.

"How long would it take us to get through all the songs?" she asked.

I'd never thought about that. "Well, assuming all the button combinations really correspond to a song, that would make it a hundred songs, and if the songs average three minutes apiece, that would be about five hours."

"What makes you think they average out to three minutes?" she asked.

"Well, that Aretha Franklin song was about two and a half, and that was a short version. Most of the time that song is closer to a full three minutes."

"How do you know?" She looked puzzled.

"It's this thing I have with music and time," I said. "I know how long a song lasts. Almost to the second. I don't know how I know. I just do." Suddenly I felt my face grow hot with embarrassment.

Her eyes brightened. "Let's start from A1 and work our way through."

Barb started feeding dimes into the jukebox, and as the songs cycled through, we talked. I'm not very good at asking people questions about themselves. In fact, I stink at it. As soon as there's a lull in a conversation, I'm stumped. *What now?* I ask myself.

That didn't seem to bother Barb. She did all the work for me, anticipating my questions before I had a chance to pose them. She told me about growing up outside of Philly, in a small college town on the Main Line. In contrast to the ceaseless whiff of tragedy that swirled around my own childhood, hers had been rich with happiness, free of all but the most minor disturbances. Her father, she said, was a slightly buttoned-up history professor from a family of Old Philadelphians, while her free-spirited mother had given up a career in dance to have the kids, then teach. She adored both her older brothers.

I sat awed. Barb was polishing off the last crumbs of my chocolate pie, scraping the plate with the back of her fork then licking the tines like a lollipop. She leaned forward.

"And you, Man of Few Words? Did you grow up in Philly?"

Ordinarily, I dread being asked questions. But when I met Barb, it was as if I'd been waiting thirty years for just the right person to pose just the right question. And here she was. I told her as much as I could. Not Philly but Minnesota. First Minneapolis, then Rochester, Minnesota, and in less than a minute I came to the part that usually stirs people's voyeuristic desire for more. I marveled at Barb's comfort with letting me stop right there. There was no "Why did your grandparents raise you?" and certainly nothing as direct as "What happened to your parents?" If she was curious, she masked it well. She looked at me as if to say, *We have time. There's no rush.*

Instead of probing more about my upbringing, she asked this: "What's the deal with the naked Furby?"

She was referring to the famously annoying electronic toy from the late '90s that I had on my desk at work. It had started out purple, but its fur was now gone, its electronics exposed, like the Visible Human exhibit. I told Barb about my moonlighting gig as a reverse engineer. Law firms representing companies embroiled in patent disputes hired me as their high-tech detective. I would take a finished product and trace it back through thousands of steps to its original specifications in order to pinpoint where an infringement might have occurred. In reverse engineering a product, I explained to her, I had to work my way through electronic circuitry to understand how the signals were used.

Barb looked amused—and puzzled. "I'm not sure I really get it," she said.

"It's like being given a slice of cake," I said, "then being told to unbake it and produce the recipe and list the raw ingredients."

"That sounds impossible," she said, shaking her head.

"I like that it's hard. Baking a cake might take a lot of skill, but unbaking a cake is a more interesting problem."

I seldom heard how a case turned out. Nor did I particularly care to find out. Legal claims around patents and trade secrets and prior art didn't interest me, but the thrill of a technical puzzle did. I started my work in forensic engineering as an undergraduate and did it on and off until I joined Rita Receptionists, programming the company's entire system from the ground up, which, from a reverse engineering standpoint, somehow felt backward.

I told Barb I'd taken apart digital cameras, printers, and laser pointers. One of my most gratifying assignments was to reverse engineer the Furby after its manufacturer, a company called Tiger Electronics, was sued for patent infringement. The Furby was a state-of-the-art achievement in compact, highly intricate, cost-effective engineering, and taking it apart to understand the inner workings was a challenge that matched the toy's complexity. I told Barb about all the hidden screws, the two-piece circuit board at the Furby's heart, and the epoxy hiding the Furby's proprietary chips.

Some other woman might have found my Furby project boring, even creepy. But Barb looked spellbound. She had her elbows on the table and her chin was resting on one palm.

"And did you unbake the Furby in the end?"

I nodded. "It took a few tries."

"How many have you deprogrammed? Or dissected? Or dismantled? Or whatever you do?"

"Five," I said.

"Do you ever do anything Frankenstein-ish to them?"

"Sometimes I reprogram them to say interesting things."

"Like what?" She was really into it.

"That's proprietary."

"Doesn't it make you sad that you're . . . killing them?" I must have looked a little shocked by the question because she caught herself. "Okay, forget I asked that."

Barb checked the song playing on the jukebox (J4: "Back in the U.S.S.R."), then held her arm up for me to read her watch, a vintage men's Omega that overwhelmed her tiny wrist. "Are we on schedule with the songs?" she asked. It was 11:05 p.m.

"Almost exactly."

She told me our jukebox experiment reminded her of a bachelor uncle of hers who'd lived in New York in the '80s. He decided one day that he was going to try each and every eating establishment listed in the 1984 Manhattan Yellow Pages, starting with A. I. Gyro, at 15 East Thirty-First Street, working his way through until he rested his knife and fork after a meal at Zulfikar Luncheonette on West Thirty-Seventh. And he was going to walk to all of them from his apartment on Broadway and Eighty-Sixth. There were thousands of restaurants; it took him seven years to conquer the list. He started out tracking his progress on green ledger sheets, eventually switching over to a Lotus spreadsheet. He logged only three categories: what he ate; the level of cleanliness, with a subcategory for whether he spotted a cockroach; and the brand of cutlery, his sole measure of elegance. I liked that uncle, sight unseen.

By midnight we'd heard only two-thirds of the jukebox songs. Barb said she was beginning to fade and suggested we finish our project another night. *Our* project. *Another night.* Elation!

But when we got outside, she appeared to have caught a second wind because she said, "I want to know what that Furby on your desk does." She insisted we go back to the office.

The story of my Furby hacks was something I'd never shared with anyone. We unlocked the office and flipped on the lights, and Barb made a beeline for my cubicle. She picked up the Furby and pushed the big round button on its tummy. No sound. Then she pulled at its ears and stuck her pinky in its plastic little mouth. Still nothing.

"Try upside down," I said.

As soon as she turned the toy on its head, the little guy launched into Pavarotti's transcendent version of "Ave Maria."

Barb seemed stunned. We stood in reverential silence while Barb held the inverted Furby through all four minutes and forty-six seconds of the tenor's performance.

"Wow," she said when it was over. "It sounds so good!"

"I gave it higher quality output than the original, basically just a better speaker."

Now that she'd broken the code on this one, Barb was examining the Furby closely, as if it might hold still more surprises. She held it with both hands, her arms outstretched, and viewed the toy appraisingly. "Does this Furby have a name?"

"No," I said.

"It needs a name," she said. "How about Strip, short for *stripped-down*?"

"Sure," I said, warming to the idea of giving my Furby an identity. "Strip."

By the time we were outside again, the buses had stopped running. Barb's place was a relatively easy walk, while mine was a couple of miles away. She asked if I was allergic to cats. When I said I wasn't sure but didn't think so, the corners of her mouth turned up in a small amused smile and she offered to let me sleep on her foldout couch.

She introduced me to her cat, named Mike the Cat, a gray longhaired feline. He was curled up on the couch when we arrived. The cat was totally mellow. He barely acknowledged us, and Barb had to shoo him off to make up my bed. When I came out of the bathroom I was touched to see that she had propped a stuffed duck against the pillow. One of its black plastic button eyes was missing.

Barb asked me if there was anything I needed.

"I guess I'm all set," I said. I was so nervous while standing there, and so unsure of myself, that all I could think to do (if I was thinking at all) was extend my hand to her. If she found that as unbefitting of the occasion as it so clearly was, she didn't let on. She shook my hand, with a saluting dip of her head, as if addressing a royal. Her grip was strong, her hand warm and soft.

When I woke up the next morning, Barb was standing over me, holding out a mug of coffee. She'd added just enough half-and-half to bring the coffee to a perfect dark caramel hue, and it struck me that over the past months she'd been watching me every bit as closely as I her. I sat up and took a sip. It was strong and delicious.

"I'm glad to see the duck made it through the night without getting reverse engineered," she said.

"No electronics," I replied. "The duck was safe."

Barb laughed, her dimples disappearing into the freckles that dusted her face, a face made still softer by the frame of her hair, freed at last from the barrette. She sat down on the edge of the sofa, took the coffee mug from my hand, and put it on the floor. Then, in a gesture no more complicated than the fixing of a stray hair, she kissed me softly on the lips. There was coffee on her breath, which made me self-conscious about my own.

"I have coffee breath," I whispered.

"So do I," she whispered back.

"Then we cancel each other out," I said.

"In more ways than one, is my guess."

"To be honest," I said, "this bed wasn't so comfortable."

"Let's give it a run for its money, and then you'll never have to sleep on it again." She kissed me again, and this time it was a delicious, lingering meeting of lips.

We made love right then and there on that too-springy sofa bed in the bright morning light, Mike the Cat curled up obliviously at the foot, the one-eyed duck bobbing as if at sea in a squall. Barb seemed touched by my shyness, deferential to my relative inexperience with skin on skin. Through adulthood and a series of crushes that went largely unrealized, my love life hadn't amounted to much. Here with Barb, I was at once gluttonous and self-conscious and tried my best to disguise both.

Girl. Cat. Duck. In that moment they became my family, suddenly populating to capacity the sad little island that had comprised my emotional landscape to date. It was then, too, that I decided that every life is allotted only one most luminous moment, and this was mine.

• • • •

My romance with Barb played out at megahertz speed, which was disorienting for a person like me, who until now had basically plodded through life. Inside of two months, I gave up my studio apartment and moved in with Barb, Mike the Cat, and the one-eyed duck. All I took with me was a suitcase filled with clothes, some computer paraphernalia, and, to Barb's delight, a box filled with Furbys.

My route to work changed, throwing me off my routine, which had consisted of a stop every morning at Happy Donut for a maple-glazed. I didn't let on to Barb how unmoored I felt without the donut. I was quietly thrilled—and decided our relationship was truly meant to be—when I discovered that Barb's neighborhood also had a Happy Donut, requiring only a small detour on my way to the bus.

I quickly grew attached to Mike the Cat, whose favorite napping spot, aside from the couch, was atop towels on a shelf of Barb's linen closet. Mike the Cat had paws the size and shape of tablespoons, all the better to sit in front of his bowl and patiently ladle milk into his mouth. It was an unusual skill for a cat, something I watched with enduring admiration.

Mike the Cat was already a senior citizen by the time I met him, a reality I had trouble adjusting to. I had never owned a pet, yet from knowing people who did I was aware that we bring animals into our lives in tacit acknowledgment of the heartbreak to come, recognizing that in the normal course of events we will eventually have to watch them grow arthritic and rheumy, then say a final, wrenching goodbye. From the minute I met Mike the Cat, I lived in fear of the day we would find him splayed on the living room rug, seized by respiratory failure or colitis or the final agonizing throes of cat cancer.

"How do cats usually die?" I asked soon after Barb introduced me to him, in an obvious confession of ignorance.

"Outdoor cats get run over a lot," she said. She saw me wince. I barely knew Mike the Cat and I was already grateful to Barb for sparing him that danger. "But since Mike the Cat is an indoor cat . . . ." She paused and scrunched her mouth pensively. "To be honest, I think just mainly old age, like people." Enough said. I took a silent vow to help Barb give Mike the Cat the best sunset to his life that a cat could hope for.

3.

If Barb hadn't come along, I'm sure my social life would have remained a pathetic zilch, and I'd have shuffled my way straight into a solitary middle age. But come along she did, and during those magical first weeks we were joined at the proverbial hip. We fell into an easy pattern of going to her apartment every night after work. I listened raptly as she described the other people in her graduate program, her seminars, the books she was reading. In turn, the talkative side of me—a side I'd never known I possessed—came alive. I'd spent a lifetime in hibernation, storing up things I wanted to share with Barb without knowing it, things like the Furby project. When Happy Donut was sold out of maple-glazed one morning, I later explained to Barb an algorithm they could use to make sure they never ran out. Or I described at some length my invention for alerting drivers if they were going to open their car doors into the paths of passing bicycles. I also had an idea for giving people their choice of music on the rare occasions they called Rita Receptionists and got placed on hold. Barb took it all in, with as much genuine interest as if I were Einstein describing special relativity. Now I felt like I could skip sleep for the next fifty years. I just wanted to natter away to her about anything that popped into my head.

She also appreciated my talent for impersonations. My favorite person to mimic was Peter Falk as Columbo, television's most humble homicide detective. I would hunch my shoulders and put one hand in a front pocket of my jeans, rubbing my chin with the other. As I began to leave a room, I would stop suddenly in the doorway and turn around to face Barb, forefinger raised. "Just one more thing, Ms. Pressman. I hate to take up more of your time, but I can't shake this nagging feeling that you look an awful lot like one of my favorite actresses. I'm just trying to remember who. It's right on the tip of my tongue."

Barb would do her best to play along.

"Oh, now it's coming back to me," and I'd slap my forehead. "Katharine Hepburn! I'm pretty sure you must be closely related to her. Granddaughter, maybe?"

Or, if we were eating out and Barb was seized by her menu-decision paralysis, Columbo would show up.

"Barb," I'd say in Columbo's gravelly tone, brandishing an invisible cigar. "Do you mind if I call you Barb?"

"Not at all, Lieutenant," Barb would reply. "How may I be of help?"

"No disrespect intended, ma'am. But I've been watching you study this menu, and I've seen your eyes keep coming back to the same thing."

"Really?"

"Again, I hope you don't think I'm taking liberties, but if I'm not mistaken, there's one dish you've been looking at more intently than the others."

"Do you have a suspect?"

"Yes, I do. This chicken mar . . . , chicken mar . . . . Sorry, my foreign pronunciation isn't so good."

"Chicken marsala!"

"Right. Chicken marsala. Now, you've looked at that item for a total of forty-two seconds, versus twenty-one seconds at the ravioli, and just a few seconds at everything else."

"The chicken marsala *is* what I keep looking at! How did you know?"

"Just my job, ma'am." I'd wink at her. After we placed our orders, I would keep the act going. "Don't get me wrong, ma'am, but I just noticed there's an escape clause in that contract you just entered into with the waiter. It's called the chocolate-cream-pie clause, and it states . . . ." I'd peer at the bottom of the menu with one eye half shut. "If your food arrives and the meal of your dining partner looks more appealing, it's all yours, no questions asked."

At work, we were careful not to advertise our relationship, but people figured it out pretty quickly. I started to get some good-natured teasing from Brendan, one of the Rita cofounders. His nickname was Brunch, his favorite meal. A former Rhodes Scholar from the University of North Carolina, Brunch was big and solid and square-jawed, a lacrosse player who took up golf once he got to Wharton. Unlike Dave, the other founder, who was a quiet numbers guy, Brunch was a fortissimist who approached life as if it were one big opportunity to crack a joke. Brunch was a serial dater who spent five minutes between girlfriends. He had charisma to spare, and it was thanks to Brunch's back-slappy, bro persona that Rita became a darling among investors. What made him most extraordinary, though, was his ability to listen. By all appearances, you'd think he'd be a verbal steamroller, one of those people who, when interrupted while saying something, just raises the volume of his own voice to drown out the interrupter, then plows ahead. But when Brunch was interrupted, he hushed up and listened, no matter how besotted he might have been with what he was saying. And I have to say, convincing venture capitalists that a startup that basically answered the phone was a sexy play required a sleight of hand that only someone with Brunch's moxie could have pulled off.

I knew I could count on Brunch to dispense with discretion when it came to Barb and me. "When's the wedding, guys?" he'd say when he saw us getting out of the elevator. Or, if he happened to catch me alone: "I guess you're a zero-to-sixty type." Yet magically somehow, Brunch knew where to draw lines, and now he seemed genuinely pleased for me.

Every Sunday, Barb went for dinner with her parents in Haverford, the tony Main Line suburb where she'd grown up, leaving Mike the Cat and me to fend for ourselves. Sunday night at her parents' was a ritual Barb had established when she returned to Philly for grad school after college. Each week, as soon as she left, I was acutely aware of her absence. I walked down to Koch's Deli for a meatball hoagie and kept wondering what she was doing and whether she missed me. It was an unfamiliar feeling, at once disconcerting and delicious, given that just a few months earlier, my sense of well-being hadn't hinged on anyone besides myself. It's so odd how you can be perfectly fine in life, just going about your days; then someone enters the picture and—wham—you're separated for a few hours and you feel like your arm has fallen off.

A few weeks later, when it came time for Barb to make her pilgrimage to Haverford, she asked if I'd like to come too. This felt like a very big step, but big steps seemed to be paying off and so I agreed.

On the train Barb told me a few more things about her family. Prep material. For one, she told me that both parents would insist on being called by their first names.

"My father is Dan, and my mother is Elizabeth . . . but everyone calls her Bunny."

"Bunny?"

"They had Elizabeth all picked out, and her nickname would have been Betsy. Even before she was born an aunt sent a silver cup with 'Betsy' engraved on it. But every day when my grandfather came to the hospital to visit, he'd say, 'How's my bunny?' Or, 'What's my little bunny up to today?' She's been Bunny ever since."

Barb told me her mother was a great cook, particularly great with vegetables grown in her own garden. "It'll be the best meal you've had in months," she said. "I'll bet you can come up with a couple of good questions for them."

Barb had decided that my phobia around starting conversations was something I could overcome. If we went out to dinner, say, with friends of Barb's, she'd suggest questions in advance. And if I managed to ask one, she'd smile proudly, as if I'd just baked a perfect soufflé. If we bumped into someone we knew, Barb whispered into my ear a question or two to ask.

"People get suspicious when someone doesn't ask them a single question about themselves," she said on the train.

"What are they suspicious of?"

"They think they're dealing with a narcissist, and you're not a narcissist. I know you're curious about other people," she said. "So just ask a question that you think might get the conversation going."

"It's not that simple," I told her.

"What's hard about it for you?"

"I'm not sure," I said. "There's something about the whole back-and-forth that makes me nervous. It's like a conversation will get started, and then I'll completely lose my mental map of where we're going, or even why we're talking at all. It's like tennis—"

She looked at me expectantly, but I didn't want to get her hopes up about me and sports, so I quickly said, "I mean, it's what tennis must feel like to people who play it. You serve the ball and then you're not sure where to stand, or what kind of shot is going to get sent back to you. It's anxiety producing."

Barb shrugged. "All you have to remember is that people love to be asked questions."

"I don't."

She ignored that. "And people love to talk about themselves. Asking one good question is like pushing the play button."

That second observation applied even to me, since meeting Barb. She would ask me the simplest question—"How was your day?"—and I was off and running. I delivered entire soliloquies.

With my having promised her I would give the question asking a try, we got off the train in Haverford and walked from the station to her parents' home, which took all of ten minutes. Barb's

parents still lived in the house where they'd raised Barb and her
two older brothers, on Railroad Avenue, a quiet street that reminded me a little of my grandparents' street back in Minnesota,
but the brick and stone houses here were more solid and a great
deal bigger. It was October, and the leaves on the majestic old
oaks and maples that lined Railroad Avenue were in the colorful
throes of autumnal demise. Houses up and down the street had
rocking chairs and porch swings. Colorful gourds lined people's
steps.

The Pressman family home was a hundred-year-old farmhouse
that had been added to over the years. It was one of the smaller
houses on the block, but it still looked huge to me. Barb's father
greeted us at the door and gave his daughter a long hug, as if he
hadn't seen her in years, although it had been a week.

"Dad, this is Ethan," Barb said, almost shyly. "Ethan, this is
Dan."

"A pleasure, Ethan," Dan Pressman said, shaking my hand.
His hand was warm and soft; I worried that mine was clammy.
His face was lean, with creases around his mouth and eyes from a
lifetime of smiling. Which was what he was doing as he looked
straight into my eyes. I shifted my weight, made uncomfortable
by his attention.

We followed our noses through the formal dining room and
into the kitchen, where Barb's mother was busy cooking. She
wiped her palms on a floral-print apron tied in a bow knot in the
front and came toward us. She and Barb pressed their cheeks together; then she turned to me and hugged me. I did my best to
reciprocate. "So nice to meet you, Ethan!"

Bunny Pressman was roughly Barb's height and wiry like her
daughter, but her face was angular where Barb's was soft and round.

The kitchen table was set for five. I felt a ripple of anxiety.

"Frank's coming," Bunny said.

"Oh, great!" Barb said. "Where's Judith?" She turned to me. "Frank's the best."

"Judith's out of town, so he's a bachelor this weekend," Bunny said.

Barb and Bunny gave me a quick rundown. Frank was an old family friend, Dan's college roommate. A lawyer for whom making money never mattered, Frank ran a nonprofit that provided legal assistance to children who were abused or neglected— clearly the work of angels. He and his wife, Judith, were Barb's godparents.

When Bunny turned down Barb's offer to help in the kitchen, Barb told me to follow her for a tour of the house. The living room was furnished comfortably, with overstuffed (but not at all stuffy) chairs and a big well-worn couch, its arms torn to shreds over the years by a series of cats.

On our way up to the second floor, we passed a row of a dozen or so clear cubes displayed on a shelf tucked into the staircase landing. The cubes were uniform in size, each with sides about three inches in length. I stopped and picked one up. Embedded in the hard plastic was a tiny toy soldier, no more than two inches long, a perfect replica of a Union infantryman.

Barb told me the story. Her great-grandfather, Dr. Charles Pressman, a renowned otolaryngologist in the early twentieth century, gained fame for his pioneering method of using an endoscope to remove foreign objects lodged in esophagi and airways, most often in small children. He'd retrieved some two thousand objects. I quickly did the math—about an object a week over a forty-year career.

"Years ago, my father decided to encase the best ones in Lucite," she said. "This is my favorite. She picked up a cube and handed it to me. Captured amber-like inside was a miniature clothes iron. "Someone swallowed that, if you can believe it," she said.

"Ouch."

"You're not kidding," Barb replied. "The rest of the collection is at the Mütter."

"The what?"

"The Mütter Museum in Philly."

I gave her a blank stare.

"It's a museum of medical oddities," she explained. "My great-grandfather had something to do with starting it. Or maybe it was just that he donated his collection. I'll take you there sometime." Barb told me she sometimes went to the Mütter to work, spreading her books and papers out on a huge old table in the library on the second floor. She said it was one of the quietest study spots in all of Philly, and it was usually empty; some of her most productive hours were spent in the Mütter library.

I was having trouble getting my mind around the concept of a museum of medical oddities, much less a place like that used as a study hall. But just as I was trying to formulate the right question about the museum, Barb moved on, leading me to the top of the stairs to see her childhood bedroom, a small window-lined room that Bunny, an expert seamstress, had turned into a sewing room. Barb didn't seem to mind the transformation in the least. To the contrary, she seemed proud at the sight of her former bedroom strewn with fabric, jagged scissors, tape measures, and pincushions. Numerous sewing projects in various stages of completion were scattered here and there. The desk held a black sewing machine marked with "Singer" in gold letters.

"That doesn't look like state-of-the-art sewing technology," I said.

"It was my grandmother's," Barb replied, patting the machine fondly.

In Haverford, a lot of things about Barb fell into place. There was the quirky side to the Pressmans, to be sure—I can't imagine there are many families with collections of objects fished out of children's throats. But I also came to understand more fully how warm and womb-like her entire upbringing had been. She was the daughter of parents who had set out to raise a family of happy people. Neither of Barb's brothers was at dinner that night— Danny, the oldest, had married a British woman and lived in London; Rob was a teacher in Pittsburgh—but evidence of their existence was everywhere: a lacrosse stick that hadn't yet made it up to the attic; photos on the refrigerator of the brothers, their wives, and a happy baby in a Beefeater T-shirt. More Pressman family photos occupied space on every available surface: the three kids, each at different ages, camping, ice skating, and just hanging out in the backyard or by a pool.

I lingered on a photo of Barb, age six or seven, standing at the end of a diving board, her arms forming a triangle above her tiny frame as one of her brothers held her at the waist from behind, teaching his little sister to dive. Barb was plainly doted upon by those boys. I had no idea what that kind of childhood felt like, but I was becoming happily aware of the result. I guess I could have been jealous, but that wasn't the feeling, exactly— though I would have traded my unusual upbringing for Barb's

in a minute. Rather, I felt privileged to be shown the way into
her world.

When we returned to the kitchen, Frank had arrived. He was
a balding, joyous, open book of a man; there was a lot of hugging
and general chatter and a perceptible rise in the energy in the
room. "Frank, this is Ethan," Barb said, reinforcing my special
status with her pointed omission of the word *friend*.

Bunny asked Frank about his latest case, which had made
national news. A fifteen-year-old girl from China had been sold
to a troupe of traveling Chinese acrobats and forced to perform
acrobatics at multiple venues a day for four years before she
escaped. Frank's organization had just found a foster family
for her.

"How awful," said Barb, horrified by the story.

Frank nodded. "Sometimes exploitation knows no limit," he
said.

When it was time for us to sit down, Bunny untied her apron,
pulled it over her head, and, with a slight ceremonial flourish,
went to hang it on a hook in the pantry. I suddenly had a vision
of Barb doing the very same thing with an apron, although I'd
never seen her wearing one. I was overcome with the oddest sen-
sation, a mash-up of premonition and déjà vu.

As Bunny spooned lamb stew onto our plates from a cast-iron
Dutch oven, I wondered how many meals she had dished out
using that long, bent pewter serving spoon, how many times the
family had eaten off these heavy white plates, some a little
chipped; I envisioned the thousandfold scraping of knives evi-
denced by small lines traversing the plates like snail tracks. The
stew had extra carrots for Barb, who, it turned out, was a huge
carrot fan. There was so much still to learn about her!

Barb's father, Dan, taught history at Haverford College. His area was modern European history, specifically the industrial revolution in England, a topic about which I knew next to nothing. Bunny was an elementary school teacher who now ran the Montessori school in town.

Bingo. My first question: "Do the kids call you Mrs. Pressman or Bunny?" It was so easy!

Bunny laughed in a way that was identical to Barb, something between a giggle and a full-throated guffaw. I noted that mother and daughter both laughed in a note that hovered around an E. "They call me Bunny," she said, her candid eyes creasing at either side. "And a few weeks ago, a little girl—she's six or seven—came up to me and said, 'Is Bunny your real name?' I said, 'No, Caitlin, my real name is Rabbit!' She loved it!"

Now Barb did the hybrid laugh. Barb's parents had a knack for asking questions in a way that didn't make me feel sized up or challenged. And no one seemed to mind that I wasn't much of a talker around people I was meeting for the first time. Knowing Barb, she'd probably warned them about this in advance. I was sure she'd said something like, "Ethan's a still-waters-run-deep type."

For dessert Bunny served a peach cobbler. It had been in the oven during dinner, and I could smell it while we ate. The dissonance of smelling something sweet while eating something savory was almost overpowering. Bunny carried the dish with the cobbler to the table with two large red oven mitts on her hands and placed it, steaming hot, on a trivet. She served it while Barb's father spooned out vanilla bean ice cream.

The cobbler was really something. Under the perfectly baked crunchy sweet crust floated thick chunks of peach, not too sweet, and definitely not canned.

"But where did you find fresh peaches in October?" I asked. Another bingo! I hadn't even had to think about that one.

"You know how you'll buy a peach at the store that looks perfect, and it feels ripe and even smells great?" said Bunny. "Then you cut into it and it's mealy and dry inside, and inedible?"

"Oh yeah," Barb said. "I hate when that happens."

"So, whenever I get mealy peaches like that, I freeze them, then make a pie or cobbler. I add a little lemon juice to moisten them up."

"What a great idea," Barb said. "Who knew?" Dan was looking adoringly at his wife.

This family now inviting me into its fold could be summed up by the steaming peach cobbler that sat before us in brightly painted bowls. Instead of being depressed by a mealy peach, Bunny Pressman viewed it as an opportunity. She took those desiccated orbs and made a delicious peach cobbler.

Occasionally I stopped to wonder what Barb could possibly see in me, socially awkward, taciturn Ethan Fawcett. Once, sensing my puzzlement, Barb ticked off a list of reasons. "I love knowing you're not someone who goes around trying out partners like cars," she said. "And who else would inspire me to do our jukebox experiment? You're just completely unlike anyone else." As soon as Barb said that, it dawned on me that she was as enamored of my otherness as I was of her breathtaking equanimity.

"And do you even know how good-looking you are?" Without waiting for an answer, she took my hand and laced my fingers through hers.

Barb and I got engaged six months after we started living together. We were sitting at the bus shelter, waiting for a bus that never arrived, in the middle of a Philly winter that wouldn't let up. We'd just had a fight. It was a rare day when we went to work at the same time, and Barb had decided it was too cold to walk. With the time saved by taking the bus, she gave herself a few extra minutes to get ready. I had the bus schedule memorized and knew we were going to miss it if she didn't hurry. I rushed her, with an unfortunate choice of words to describe her delay in getting out the door—"lollygagging"—which made her angry.

Mostly, I was put out that I'd sacrificed the extra five to seven minutes I needed for my Happy Donut detour. It was late March but as frigid and windy as deep January. Barb sat at the other end of the narrow flip-down aluminum bench at the bus stop, hunched against the cold, the hood of her navy down parka obscuring all but her delicate nose. She was so small I couldn't begin to imagine how she stayed warm. *Hummingbirds have it easier than this person*, I thought.

We sat silently. The next bus was due in twelve minutes but we'd already been waiting for fifteen. I had a hunch that this might not be an optimal occasion for asking her to marry me, but I'd been carrying the ring around for two weeks. I didn't see the point of engineering something hokey like a romantic dinner or a skywriting plane. I wanted to scoot over on that bench, fold her into my arms, and be her human heater. Given the fight, that seemed out of the question.

I offered her my scarf. "You look like you could use some help in the warmth department," I said. "Maybe on a permanent basis."

She took the scarf, and when she began to loop it around her neck, the small gray box embossed with the jeweler's name tumbled to the ground. She bent to pick it up, then suddenly swiveled her head toward me, reached up with her free arm, and pulled me into a kiss. Faintly, distantly, I heard a loud sigh—it was the bus doors opening. Then closing again. The bus pulled away, but we didn't notice. We were too busy admiring the diamond on her finger, and the way it caught the light, even on a gray, sunless day.

4.

IT WAS WHILE WORKING AT RITA RECEPTIONISTS THAT BARB got the idea for her PhD dissertation: the effects of loneliness on the elderly. She swore she could tell when someone on the other end of the line was lonely. The caller seldom, if ever, admitted it, but I could tell that those calls lasted longer, quickly veering off topic.

Barb knew that people who called regularly were lonely. Some called every day, asked for Barb, and made a point of asking how Mike the Cat was doing. They also asked after that young man of hers, the one with the special affection for the cat. Then they would launch into a soliloquy about the various setbacks and joys (but mostly setbacks) in their own lives. Barb didn't mind lingering on those calls—she thought it was the least she could do. And to their credit, the company's two founders, for whom efficiency was king, didn't object to the fact that Barb's calls sometimes lasted five, or even ten, minutes longer than our productivity algorithms stipulated.

Barb noticed that most of her lonely callers sounded older. As a psychologist, she was intrigued, and it led her to start investigating the link between loneliness and age. She quickly gravitated to the work of a Dutch sociologist named Jenny de Jong Gierveld, whose research focused on the health effects of loneliness. Professor Gierveld often invoked the concept of a personal "convoy"—a collection of family, friends, social contracts, work, passions, and pastimes that accompany us through a lifetime. With the passing of years, ships in the convoy gradually fall away, until we find ourselves facing the quiet devastation of loneliness.

When Barb told me about the disappearing convoy, I imagined a vast ocean dotted with millions of small dinghies bobbing in isolation, each containing a solitary person, a melancholy image if ever there was one.

In the course of her research, Barb learned of Silver Line, a nonprofit in the United Kingdom that had set up a hotline for lonely elders to call at any time of day or night. Practically from the time the service went live, Silver Line's phones didn't stop ringing.

We'd been engaged for a couple of months when Barb decided to take her dissertation research to Blackpool, a down-at-the-heels resort on the west coast of England, north of Liverpool, and home to Silver Line's call center. Barb's plan, supported with enthusiasm by her thesis advisor, was to do a six-month field study to determine the psychological benefits (if any) of a call-in center for socially isolated older people. This meant an extended stay in the UK. I tried not to tip my hand to Barb, but the thought of her in a place that sounded so remote it might just as easily have been Antarctica made me panic. I've always been a little bit on the vigilant side when it comes to personal safety, but this level of nervousness surprised even me. I took it as a sign of the depth of my feelings for Barb.

"Where will you stay?" I asked.

"It's all worked out," she said. "There's a staff member who has an extra bedroom in her house."

"How will you get back and forth every day?"

"I haven't thought about that yet," she said. "I'll probably drive with her."

"What if you go at different hours?"

"I'm sure there are buses."

"I'm not sure I like the sound of that. Take a taxi. I'll pay for it."

"I'll be fine. I'll email you multiple times a day," she said. "And you can come visit!"

Visit? How could I possibly leave Mike the Cat? His health was reaching a critical juncture. He was sixteen now, and increasingly blind. And he'd been wheezing a lot, or doing something I interpreted as a wheeze, and began to meow in a way that sounded like a newborn's wail, existential in its force.

"He's always been a loud crier" was Barb's response. I also worried he might have some dementia setting in, exacerbated by his visual impairment. He began to wander up to the wall of a room and cry that desperate cry of his until one of us turned him around and pointed him in the opposite direction. So even a few days at Cat's Cradle, the cat hotel in our neighborhood, seemed too risky.

"Who would take care of him?" I asked.

"That's why God invented cat sitters."

Barb was touched by my concern for Mike the Cat, which she considered genuine, but she guessed that my real reason for not wanting to visit her was my general aversion to traveling. The subject of travel had come up a few weeks into our relationship during that interminable Philadelphia winter, when we looked out the window one morning to see that freezing rain had turned the sidewalks and streets into one flat sheet of ice. Barb suggested we take a long weekend and fly down to Florida, where a couple of her college friends now lived. I balked.

My reasons beyond the cat for refusing to go to Florida—too hot and muggy there, too busy at work—failed to satisfy her. I think she sensed a backstory that I was loath to reveal. And while I felt a certain obligation to disclose to her more than I already had, I found myself tongue-tied.

One night before Barb left for England we went to Miss Flo's Diner after work. We'd become regulars. The cashier kept an extra roll of dimes in the cash register, just for us, and we continued to work our way through the songs on the jukebox at what we called "our booth." But recently we'd been taking it much more slowly, playing only a song or two per seating. Barb grew superstitious, wondering whether hitting the last song would bring bad luck. "We'll move to another booth and start all over again," I said cheerfully.

Once we had settled into our booth, Barb surprised me by saying she was curious about my childhood. And to my greater surprise, I took her comment—which I knew was actually a question—in stride. The safety I had come to associate with Miss Flo's struck me as a setting as good as any for filling in some biographical blanks.

My mother, I told her, was a computer programmer. She worked at a big Minneapolis computer company called Control Data Corporation, or CDC (and not the CDC that's been all over the news these days). As a child, I was sure she ran the place, but I learned years later that she was deep in the ranks, a senior programmer working in a dialect of Fortran, the programming language famous for its IF statements. She often spoke Fortran to me, our private language, as my father looked on, amused and befuddled by our IF-THEN-ELSE logic:

```
IF (it is raining today) THEN
     TAKE (= 1 umbrella)
ELSE
     WEAR (= 1 rain jacket)
END IF
```
or this:
```
IF (a parent fails to pick you up after school) THEN
     GO TO (office and ask them to call)
ELSE
     (continue to wait)
END IF
```
or this:
```
IF (you run off to join the circus) THEN
     PACK (underwear >= one week)
ELSE
     LOCATE (laundromat <= 0.5 miles)
END IF
```

I told Barb that I had sharp images in my mind's eye of accompanying my mother to work on weekends, when no one else was around, and marveling at those massive machines kept behind glass. Though I was too young to understand the technical underpinnings of her work, something must have stuck because, well, here I am, the proverbial (micro)chip off the block that was my mother the programmer.

My father was an artist, the poetic weft threading through my mother's stolid warp. He was a sculptor who made pieces I never really understood.

"I do assemblage," he once told me. He liked to repurpose objects he found on the street—glass bottles, pieces of metal, cardboard, even the occasional piece of furniture left out on a sidewalk. His studio was in our garage, and I remember a jumble of junk; he spent hours telling me where he'd found things.

His day job was at the Walker Art Center, where he worked as a preparator. He inhabited the world of art logistics, doing everything from framing pieces to overseeing installations. He designed and built shipping crates, bases, and vitrines for three-dimensional pieces like sculptures and books and ceramics. And he was an expert lighter, with a reputation for always getting the lighting just right. When special exhibits came to town, the artist in question requested that Mark Fawcett and only Mark Fawcett do the lighting.

When my father had to stay late at the museum preparing for an exhibit, my mother packed sandwiches and some Pecan Sandies—her favorite cookie, and therefore mine—and we drove to the museum for a picnic on the polished marble floor. The highlight of these evenings was when my father gave me my own pair of white cotton gloves and took me up in the cherry picker when he had to set the lights on a particularly large painting. For years after I was sustained by the lingering perfume of this previous life.

Barb was listening to what I was saying with her chin propped on an open palm.

"What happened to your parents?" she asked, so softly I almost didn't hear the question.

I was already feeling pretty exhausted but decided to take the leap. "It happened when they were on vacation in Hawaii. My mother went swimming and got caught in a riptide. My father went in to get her. I think, I mean I hope . . . I'm pretty sure it happened quickly. But that's all I know. They were there one minute and gone the next."

Here was her opening, her chance to grill me on the details. Was I there when it happened? If not, was I nearby? Even I, with my aversion to questions, could think of a dozen logical follow-ups. But she held back.

"Are you frightened of the ocean now?" she asked. Her eyes were damp. She reached across the table and took my hand.

"I don't really know," I said. I'd never been to a beach.

I tacked abruptly in a different direction, hoping Barb wouldn't notice. My parochialism, I told her, took root on the day in 1992 that I went, at age eight, from Minneapolis to Rochester, to live with my grandparents, which happened to be the day of my parents' funeral. My grandparents filled two suitcases with my clothes and a few small toys (I insisted on taking my Model HO railroad set, and to my great relief they complied) and drove me straight back to Rochester.

At the height of the drama—the bleak scurrying of all the wrecked adults around me, the hasty arrangements to bury two people at the same time, the uninterrupted and solicitous, if also clumsy, torrent of attention I received—I pictured the opening scene of *Doctor Zhivago*, which my mother and I had watched on television not long before the accident. In the film, the young Yuri Zhivago, perhaps only a year or two younger than me, stands above his mother's grave, confused and bereft but stoic as can be. I recall little about what I was wearing, but I do remember a tie that clipped to my collar with a tiny hook that I couldn't attach. Frustrated, I had left it dangling from a buttonhole until an adult came along and fixed it.

Like Yuri, I was a model of composure. I didn't cry, which was all the more impressive with so many bawling people around. I imagined myself being whisked away by a couple as young and brimming with life as my own parents—just like the pair that adopted Yuri. We would travel in an S-shaped horse-drawn sleigh to a city just like Moscow and arrive at a palatial home filled with chintz and hearths, good cheer, and hundreds of toys, and I would be introduced to my new "sister"—a winsome Tanya-like girl who would love me like a sibling, and then, since we weren't actually related by blood, we would marry and be blissfully happy.

But the reality was something very different. Instead of that fairy tale, I was ushered into my grandparents' Dodge Dart, its muffler badly in need of replacing, my grandfather's face partly obscured by his newsboy flat cap as he gripped the steering wheel with his hands locked perfectly at ten o'clock and two o'clock for the entirety of the 1.5-hour drive to the white two-story house at 1313 Second Street NW in Rochester, Minnesota.

My grandparents were both research scientists at the Mayo Clinic. My grandfather was a cell biologist who did cancer research, trying to get to the bottom of what made cancer cells different from normal cells. My grandmother had both an MD and a PhD, which impresses me to this day. One of the first female nephrologists in the country, maybe the world, she studied kidney stones and discovered the role dehydration plays in causing them. I've always made a point of keeping a bottle of water close at hand and tried to impress on Tommy and Sam the importance of staying hydrated (though their delicate constitutions reject excess water).

When we arrived, my grandmother escorted me up to the familiar bedroom that had been my mother's when she was growing up. My mother had often marveled that it hadn't changed one scintilla since she was a child. A four-poster bed was covered with an afghan crocheted in the red-and-black school colors of John Marshall High. Tacked to the bulletin board above the small wooden desk were a blue ribbon in baton twirling and programs from plays that My Mother the Thespian had performed in 1963: *Babes in Arms*; *The Crucible*. In a manila envelope marked "school stuff" was a report card from her sophomore year (all As and A-minuses, with the notable exception of a C-plus in typing), along with her National Merit Scholar certificate.

On a low built-in bookshelf sat a small collection of volumes I would come to know intimately: *To Kill a Mockingbird*, *Great Expectations*, *The Diary of Anne Frank*, *The Great Gatsby*, *Anna Karenina*. The margins were filled with notes she'd made in class, in microscopic hand. A few of the books had obviously been read, but their pages were unmarked. Those were the ones I assumed my mother had read for pleasure: *Sons and Lovers*; *Marjorie Morningstar*; *I Capture the Castle*, a hardcover so dog-eared and worn I guessed she'd read it multiple times.

For the eleven years I lived in that Pompeii of a bedroom, I didn't change a thing. Nor did my grandparents offer to clean the room out, a gesture that would have allowed me to transform it into a place of my own. So my possessions came to coexist with my mother's: my prized train set alongside her old dollhouse; my baseball bat in a wicker basket next to her baton. In her yearbook, which I studied with some intensity, I saw that the high school band included a girl—Sally Nesbit—who played the tuba. Above the picture, with an arrow pointing down at a girl and her tuba, Sally wrote, "To Sheila, a cute kid and the best majorette at J.M. High!" My mother was one of ten majorettes, four of whom were boys, and tucked inside the yearbook were a dozen or so photos of her plying her craft, her face infused with sweetness. She was slightly scrawny, in knee socks, saddle shoes, and a plaid jumper. Always a jumper.

Somehow it seemed oddly comforting that I was still living with my mother, who now, in the form of her ghost, felt less like my mother and more like my older sister. It was hard to square the baton-twirling Sheila Steinhauer with the adult Sheila Steinhauer, as no evidence of my mother beyond adolescence ever made it into that bedroom. I found solace in pretending that she had never had a life beyond high school, that her ambitions had begun and ended with the John Marshall High School marching band, her career as a majorette the apogee of her time on this earth.

I stopped short of telling Barb the story I had so often told my younger self: If my mother never got beyond high school, she couldn't die. In order for that to have happened, she—and Sally and all the other Marshall High kids—*had* to be suspended in time. This was how I constructed a membrane, however tenuous, between what I knew to be true and everything else. This thought lingered for years in my mind, in the strange space between fantasy and reality.

"Did you go to that high school too?" Barb asked.

"Yes," I said. When I got there, three decades after my mother, the only teacher who remained from my mother's time was Mrs. Fitzpatrick, the tenth-grade English teacher. A much younger Mrs. Fitzpatrick had signed my mother's yearbook: "Dear Sheila, thank you for all your lively contributions to the class. Never stop reading! Mary Fitzpatrick."

Mrs. Fitzpatrick still assigned all those old chestnuts, the books that filled my bedroom. Despite my growing love of programming, I looked forward to English class like no other, carrying my mother's annotated books on daily pilgrimages to school and removing them from my backpack with quiet reverence—for my mother, for Mrs. Fitzpatrick, for the books themselves.

My hunch is that my grandparents hadn't really thought twice about the fact that I was sharing a bedroom with the material vestiges of my mother's childhood; they even continued to see it as her room. Say I'd be hunting for a sweatshirt. "Last time I saw it, it was in Sheila's room," my grandmother would say.

At the dinner table, my grandparents talked mostly about work, about their research grants and their colleagues' research grants, about the new article in such-and-such medical journal or the paper they were reviewing for such-and-such other journal. In other words, I heard a lot more about the logistics of science than science itself, which made me decide early in college to avoid research as a career and find something more practical, much as my mother had.

My grandparents shared an abiding passion for classical music. Something was always on the record player, before work, after work, and through the weekend. My grandfather, an amateur oboist who played in a local chamber ensemble, gravitated to pieces heavy on woodwinds, while my grandmother preferred the dramatic late Beethoven string quartets. They both loved Bach, especially Glenn Gould's two recordings—separated by twenty-five years—of the Goldberg Variations, which they often listened to back-to-back.

Both of my grandparents emerged from their customary taciturn shell whenever they talked about music. My grandmother grew especially animated when she told me about having seen Gould perform with the Rochester Symphony in the mid-1950s, when my mother was too young to accompany them. The day after the concert, my grandmother bumped into the pianist in a hall of the Mayo Clinic. Famously hypochondriacal, Gould was there for a full workup. My grandmother asked for his autograph, and he obliged, signing a cafeteria napkin she produced from her pocket.

My mother also came to admire Gould's genius, quirks and all. Gould often hummed as he played, and as a young teenager, my mother sent a letter to Columbia Records to say she had just listened to a recording of Gould playing Bach's French suites. "Now, you're not going to believe this," she wrote, "but someone is singing in the background as Mr. Gould is playing!" The record company wrote back: "Dear Miss Steinhauer, thank you for your very perceptive letter. You have excellent hearing. The singer to whom you refer is Mr. Gould himself." My grandparents framed the letter and hung it above the piano, together with the autographed napkin.

When I came to live with them, they added me to their season tickets to the Rochester Symphony. I squirmed a lot, as I longed to be swinging a baseball bat. (I was passionate about the game, if also singularly incompetent at it.) But I also strove to be a good companion for this, their sole pleasure outside of work. In the car one night after a concert that included Beethoven's Sixth, I somehow managed to hum the entire first movement, imitating the instruments as I went: the low undulating strings; the sweetness of the short oboe passage; the playful exchange between the bassoon and violins. I synched the whole thing to the ten-minute drive home and hit the final notes just as we were pulling into the driveway. "Ethan, my goodness, what an ear you have," my astonished grandmother said; then she turned to my grandfather. "He has perfect pitch, just like you, Murray." They didn't link the statement to my mother's musical talent, which was a nice change. But my grandmother did ask, "Did Sheila know you could do this?" I couldn't remember whether my mother did or not, so quickly were my more granular memories of her fading. But I couldn't bring myself to tell them this. "Yes," I lied. "It made her very proud and happy."

It was from my grandparents that I picked up a strong antipathy to travel. For one thing, they were both dedicated to their work, a calling they deemed far higher and more compelling than a trip to Paris could ever be. Also, they didn't see the point of putting themselves through the steps required to plan a trip, then actually embark on it. When I asked my grandmother about it, she said they both had a terrible time with jet lag. Even daylight savings seemed to throw them for a loop. This was all a little strange, since they weren't lazy people, and they clearly had a layer of resilience that helped them get on with life despite unspeakable tragedy. But I came to accept it for what it was, and it meant that my upbringing tended toward the insular.

By all indications, my grandparents were singularly devoted (with the exception of their work) to the task of raising my mother, their only child. But when it came to me, they seemed, well, tired. I'd bring home a report card flush with As—including an A-plus in music theory—and my grandfather would simply smile and say, "We wouldn't have expected any less of Sheila's son." Yet I didn't mind. I didn't know much about grief, but I could tell that my grandparents had been hit by something akin to a tornado, something from which they would never fully recover. Though neither of them could be described as gregarious, before they lost their daughter they were happy, dutiful grandparents. Whenever they arrived in Minneapolis for a visit, they brought gifts—books, mostly—and drove me to my T-ball, then Little League, practice. When we visited them in Rochester, I felt like a prince. I once overheard my grandmother say to my mother, "Sheila, my job with you was to be a parent. With Ethan, my job is to spoil him rotten." And my mother laughed and replied, "It's a good thing you don't live with us, Mom."

After my parents died, my presence in my grandparents' lives seemed to bring them more pain than joy. My grandfather, in particular, became a husk of a person. All of which made me all the more grateful to them for taking me in in the first place. I didn't know my father's parents, who'd both died before I was born. So, despite what I perceived as my grandparents' benign neglect, I was thankful that I hadn't ended up in an orphanage.

Extrapolating from my sample of two, I believed that all scientists led simple, somewhat dull lives, entirely free of distraction. It came as a surprise to me years later to hear about research scientists who drove shiny Volvos, lived in large houses, threw dinner parties, and took vacations.

My grandmother's favorite time at the Clinic was over the winter holidays, when she said she got her best thinking done, free of distractions. For my grandfather, he was most productive during the summer. When my grandparents did take time off, they stayed at home, working their way down a list of deferred home repairs, tending the garden, and reading books about complicated topics like supply-side economics and the history of ancient Rome. A vacation that would take us beyond a Saturday-afternoon tour of Mayowood, Charlie Mayo's forty-room mansion and extensive gardens, was out of the question. So, until the day I ventured east for college in Pennsylvania, I had lived a life roughly circumscribed by the city limits of Rochester, Minnesota.

After this stretch of monologue, I felt spent. It was the most I'd ever talked about myself. I was interested, in a clinical kind of way, to note what I chose to tell Barb that night in the diner and what I chose to withhold. There wasn't really any rhyme or reason to it. Why, for instance, did I tell her so much about my mother's favorite books? Or about my fantasies about being a real-life version of young Yuri Zhivago?

I didn't tell her that while growing up, I sometimes climbed a pull-down ladder in the back hallway that led to a small attic filled with boxes. My grandparents had saved every scrap of paper related to my mother's childhood: her letters home from summer camp; poems she wrote in first grade displaying an affinity for butterflies; essays from junior high. A box I happened upon during one of my forensic explorations contained various official-looking documents, among them a 1954 bill of sale for my grandparents' house, conveying 1313 Second Street NW to my grandparents for the grand sum of $5,875. The sellers were listed as Dr. and Mrs. Benjamin Spock. Under that document was a book, a hardcover, its dust jacket perfectly intact, titled *The Common Sense Book of Baby and Child Care*. Inside was an inscription: "To Murray and Bernice, the very fortunate new parents of Miss Sheila Steinhauer. You know more than you think you do! Warmly, Ben Spock." I tucked the book under my arm, took it down to my mother's room, and began to read it. On many of the pages, my grandmother had made notes in the margin that reinforced my appreciation of her programmatic approach to everything she did.

When I moved to Philly for college, Dr. Spock's parenting primer was the one book I took with me. My decision to confer constant companionship on that particular volume could have been due to the personal inscription, all the underlining, and the notes in the margins. Or perhaps I harbored a vague hope that Dr. Spock's wisdom might help me work through my own fear of having children. In the story I told Barb, I studiously avoided the part about lonely days spent in the cramped attic, kept company by boxes full of my grandparents' memorabilia—an image I feared she might find a little too pathetic.

I've rewound that conversation in our booth at the diner dozens of times in my mind over the past two years. If I'd told Barb the full story then and there—a story that went well beyond a lonely boy in an attic, a story that went further back, to that little boy's selfish and destructive act—might things have turned out differently for us? How did I manage to give her so little to work with? And how was it that I couldn't tell Barb everything but was able to tell Izzy—a near stranger on the payroll of Hill and Dale Adventures, whose job it was to keep me company?

It could have been that with Barb there was just too much at stake. No love is unconditional, and as much as we cherished each other, this was a confession I couldn't risk. And once the chance passed, it vanished for good, like missing someone's name at the initial introduction and being too embarrassed to admit weeks later that you still didn't know the most basic thing about that person.

I did make a stab at articulating to Barb that one byproduct of my childhood was that I came to dislike travel as much as my grandparents did, and that I even came to equate it, or any movement outside the routine, with lack of control, even outright danger. Barb might not have been listening closely enough, or perhaps she was listening selectively. After all, this was still in the early, heady days of our relationship, when infatuation trumped sober assessment, when she listened to everything I said with love-kissed interest. "You're a pearl," she said. "You're this beautiful object formed from all the grit inside the oyster shell." I may have become a pearl in her eyes, but I definitely wasn't free of grit. That much I knew.

5.

TRUE TO HER WORD, BARB EMAILED ME EVERY DAY FROM England with notes from the field. She told me about Deborah, the Silver Line staff member whose calls Barb listened in on. Deborah, she said, was a single mother in her thirties whom Barb described as the most empathic person she'd ever met (though I found it hard to imagine a more empathic person than Barb). Many of the calls on the loneliness hotline were heartbreaking, but sometimes they were entertaining. There was the caller in his eighties who took Deborah and Barb on a nostalgic trip down his list of favorite films. Another spoke eloquently about being trapped on the beach at Dunkirk in 1940, awaiting rescue. One caller serenaded a Silver Line staffer with "Oh, What a Beautiful Mornin'" on his harmonica. Pamela was a regular who called every day, and if her call wasn't picked up by Deborah, she redialed until it was.

Sometimes Barb called me after returning to the room where she was staying to tell me about a particularly upsetting call.

These were mostly conversations that occurred not because some-one called Silver Line but because Silver Line had called to check in with them. There was one woman, Beryl, whose phone call would haunt Barb for months afterward. When Deborah called Beryl one afternoon to see how she was, Beryl said she'd just spent her eighty-first birthday alone. Her voice quavered as she told Deborah that this was the first time she'd spoken in more than a week. Barb was weeping quietly while she told me about lonely Beryl and the saints of Silver Line.

Blackpool seemed safe enough (though I instructed her not to walk the streets at night or, under any circumstances, to drive a car). But on weekends, when she ventured to London to see her brother and sister-in-law and their new baby, I worried con-stantly. During one phone call before a London jaunt, I offered a few tips.

"Do you know which way to look when crossing a street?" I asked.

"Yes, and it's even written on the street which way to look."

"If someone asks you what time it is, don't look at your watch. They just want to distract you long enough for their partner to pick your pocket."

"How do you know these things? You've never even been to London."

I sent her a list: Avoid large crowds, especially in an enclosed place. People hit the pubs at 5:00 p.m. straight after work, so avoid the Underground after 8:00 p.m. because that's when all the drunk people get on. In fact, whenever you ride the Under-ground, stay away from the edge of the platform.

"When you're reading the news, do your eyeballs just gravitate to all the disasters?"

"Barb, it's the other way around. Finding news that isn't about this or that disaster is hard work."

"You're right," she conceded, or perhaps she was humoring me. "But don't worry. I'm going to be fine. And Danny's neighborhood is safe."

While Barb was gone, I went solo to Sunday dinner at her parents'. When they asked me, I hesitated—were they just being nice?—but then realized that the offer was genuine. Her brother Rob had moved back to the Philly area, and he was there every week now too. Rob was a real fan of ice hockey, a game I'd followed closely in Minnesota but had lost track of since moving to Philly. I started going to Haverford a little early so that we could watch games together, especially if the Flyers were playing. It was fun watching sports with another guy. I surprised myself by hooting in celebration when Claude Giroux, the team's standout center, scored a winning goal in overtime.

When Barb returned, fully intact, I was thrilled. But she remained adamant on the matter of travel. "Ethan, you can't spend the rest of your life hiding from experience," she said. "And in order to have experiences, sometimes you just have to get on a plane and go somewhere." I wanted to tell her I had traveled plenty, thanks to my mother's books. I'd seen Moscow and Saint Petersburg, Amsterdam, the East Egg of Long Island, Scarlett O'Hara's Atlanta, and parts of England. But I sensed she wouldn't buy it. Traveling in the pages of books, seeing the world through the eyes of a bunch of long-gone writers, wasn't enough. If we were going to make a life together, I would need to muster my courage and face the world.

6.

It was Barb's idea to get married at the Mütter Museum.

"They do weddings?" I asked.

"Yes!" she said. "My parents even celebrated their twenty-fifth anniversary at the Mütter!"

Barb took me to the Mütter one rainy Saturday morning so I could see it for myself. On the way, she offered a little tutorial on this one-of-a-kind repository of medical oddities, telling me about Dr. Thomas Mütter, a collector of unique specimens who established the museum in 1858. Barb's great-grandfather had been a student of Dr. Mütter's, and the two had shared a love of collecting.

As soon as we walked in the door, sure enough, carved permanently into the wall of the marble-lined foyer was great-grandfather Pressman's name, one of a handful of founding benefactors. The building was big—it also housed the College of Physicians of Philadelphia—but the museum itself was small. And crowded.

"The Mütter is on a lot of people's Philly bucket list," Barb told me proudly. "Right after Independence Hall, the Liberty Bell, the Italian Market, and the Rocky statue."

She made an appointment with someone named Yvette to take us around. A twenty-something event coordinator, Yvette was waiting for us at the ticket counter when we arrived, and she greeted us with a dainty, limp handshake, strangely incongruous with her exaggerated friendliness. Yvette handed each of us her business card and an events brochure. "The Mütter Museum," it read. "The Cure for the Common Wedding." Below the heading was a picture of a shelf lined with skulls. On the back of the brochure: "Are You Ready to be Disturbingly Informed?" I wasn't so sure.

I understood within a few seconds of meeting Yvette that the Mütter gave all descendants of Great-Grandfather Pressman white-glove treatment, even if they didn't quite remember the connection. "I'm a huge admirer of your uncle!" Yvette said, with extravagant good cheer.

Barb didn't seem bothered by Yvette's having gotten the Pressman family tree totally wrong. She told Yvette that as a child she had spent many a happy Saturday afternoon at the museum and had practically memorized the label on each exhibit.

"This is Ethan's first time here," Barb said. "Maybe we could show him the permanent exhibit first?"

"Yes, of course!" chirped Yvette.

This, I can tell you, was a museum like no other.

Appropriately enough, our tour started with the Pressman Collection. The plaque at the entryway to the room described Dr. Pressman, with a particular emphasis on his approach to kids.

"Possessed of an exquisite gentleness" (I saw how that trait ran true and strong in the family, showing up now in his twenty-five-year-old great-granddaughter), "Dr. Pressman encouraged children to tolerate the endoscope without benefit of anesthesia or sedation by suggesting they think of themselves as sword-swallowers," it said.

Dr. Pressman's quest was to make people conscious about their swallowing and to impress upon them the importance of thoroughly chewing their food. "Chew your milk!" he exhorted the public, memorably. With the exception of the things embedded in Lucite cubes at Barb's parents', all the objects he recovered from noses, pharynxes, and esophagi were now at the Mütter: nails, bolts, open safety pins, and charms, one in the shape of a dog, another a tiny pair of binoculars.

Barb told us how much the museum had changed since she was a child, when the specimens floated in dusty glass jars on crude wooden shelving that reached far above her head. I was charmed. The layout of the exhibits was neat and tidy, in stark contrast to the havoc wrought upon the human body that the exhibits illustrated.

We left the Pressman Room and moved into the main exhibit hall, where all the grotesqueries were on display. We glided past a jaw tumor removed from President Grover Cleveland and the conjoined livers of Chang and Eng, the famous Siamese twins, only to stop at a glass case containing a massively dilated forty-pound colon harvested from a man afflicted with chronic constipation.

Just as Barb and Yvette were discussing the relative merits of holding the ceremony outside in the medicinal plant garden or upstairs in the grand medical library, we came upon an exhibit that stopped me in my tracks.

It was the skeleton of Harry Eastlack, whose rare bone disease—the scientific name, *fibrodysplasia ossificans progressiva*, said it all—causes bones to grow in places they have no business being. Muscles, ligaments, tendons—all turn to bone. Even the lifeless skeleton, with fragments of bones attached to everything like bark to a tree, looked like it was in terrible pain. Included in the exhibit was a series of photos of Harry at age thirteen. He was naked but for a loincloth, his body already a research subject. He was so thin it looked like the skeleton was getting a head start on things, on a completely different timetable from Harry's mind and soul and beating heart. By the age of fifteen, the exhibit description said, his jaw had fused shut. At twenty-five, bone had colonized most of his body, and he spent the last dozen years of his life literally locked in place. How can the body turn so violently against itself? Yet it was Harry himself who had bequeathed his skeleton to the Mütter so that researchers could study it to better understand his disease. A sudden surge of kinship with Harry came over me. It was as if I harbored my own ossification, not of the bones but of the soul. Yet here I stood, next to Barb, the agent sent to reverse its course. I began to feel light-headed. The wooden floor felt like it might buckle beneath my feet. I steadied myself for a few moments, closing my eyes and pressing my palms to the cool glass that held Harry's skeleton. Then I looked for Barb. She was across the room, chatting with Yvette. And she was beaming. She had spent so much time at the Mütter, it's possible that the horror simply failed to register. But it took everything I had to look enthusiastic. What to me was the stuff of nightmares tapped directly into Barb's sentimental sweet spot. As we stood pondering the logistics of passed hors d'oeuvres, it became crystal clear that Barbara Ann Pressman's fondest wish was to be married in this place she knew and loved. Despite my ambivalence, I loved her all the more for that.

As for Yvette, the more gruesome the exhibit, the more upbeat she became. It seemed there was nothing at the Mütter she couldn't perkify. "We'll make sure that your guests can roam around the halls," she assured us.

It wasn't until we started putting the guest list together that Barb fully appreciated how short my own list was. Aside from my grandparents, who, I told Barb, were likely too infirm to make the trip, there were no relatives I could think to invite.

Barb was genuinely concerned. "Not even a cousin or two?" she asked. "Weren't they at family gatherings?" By this I assumed she meant funerals, the only kind of family gathering I knew. The heartbreaking tact of the question made me wish my answer could be something more satisfying than what I was able to give her.

"I suppose so," I said, my mind's eye flashing briefly on members of the Steinhauer and Fawcett clans, but more as clusters of people than as individuals. "I guess we just weren't much of an extended family." Even as I said those words, I knew I was dead wrong, that there were Steinhauers and Fawcetts peppered all over the place, whooping it up on a regular basis at weddings and christenings and bar mitzvahs and anniversaries. In point of fact, for a few years I had received invitations from both sides of the family—not just to the big milestones and reunions but to fiftieth birthdays and Thanksgivings. But I found even these happy events impossible to attend, because my first reaction at the very thought of a family get-together was an abysmal sadness. Whenever I received one of the hand-addressed envelopes with a return address I knew to be from relatives, I put it in a drawer, unopened. I couldn't throw them away, but I couldn't bring myself to open them either. After a while, they stopped coming.

Barb got it into her head that my grandparents should come to the wedding. All my excuses—they're too feeble, too averse to travel, would have no one to talk to, nowhere to stay—she dismissed out of hand. Barb sent them an invitation. I was shocked when she showed me their RSVP card with a check next to the "yes," they'd be delighted to come. "Your grandmother wants the salmon and your grandfather wants the chicken," Barb announced, as if that were the news. She found a hotel for them that was practically next door to the Mütter, and Barb's mother offered to make sure they were well looked after.

Barb and I went to the airport the day before the wedding to pick them up. I hadn't seen them for a few years, and the sight of them standing outside baggage claim was a little startling. My grandfather, even shorter than I remembered, wore his familiar flat cap. My grandmother looked smaller, too, and both were diminished further by their bulky Samsonite powder-blue suitcase, with a rope tied around it for reinforcement. My grandmother was clutching a large carpetbag with both hands in a way that made her look like a young girl on a train platform. They appeared bewildered. I hugged each of them tentatively, but Barb's hugs were exuberant and managed to crack their midwestern reserve, leaving them both smiling.

Barb's only pre-wedding request of me was that I get new eyeglasses. She wasn't a stickler for fashion, but she really disliked my oval wire rims, claiming they made me look owlish and a bit sinister. I didn't give much thought to eyewear, but Barb had definite opinions on the subject. That's because Dave and Brunch, the Rita cofounders, had two good friends from Wharton who'd started an online eyeglass frame company. The Rita staff quickly became the startup's beta testbed. Everyone at Rita with a visual impairment—and even some with perfect vision who thought the whole thing was cool—started walking around in trendy eyeglasses with pretentious names, like Maynard, or perfectly fine names with pretentious spellings, like Jacquie, and the glasses became a big topic of discussion around the office. Barb picked one out for me: a tortoiseshell pair named Hayden. "Bookish and modern, yet classic!" she said when I put them on. The glasses pinched the back of my right ear and kept slipping down the bridge of my nose. Still, it was gratifying to see that such a small thing could make Barb so happy. I thought little of it at the time, but in retrospect I wonder if the eyeglass upgrade might have been an early sign from Barb that she wanted me to be something more, or different.

With the exception of my grandparents, the wedding was a strictly Pressman affair. Gentle and avuncular Frank, Barb's godfather and family friend, officiated. I became as much a curiosity as the specimens under glass. I overheard a gaggle of young cousins sizing me up: "Nerdy in the cutest possible way!" During the ceremony, when Frank asked us about cherishing and respecting and seeing and hearing each other, instead of "I do," we both gave a resounding "I will!"

In her wisdom, Barb seated my grandparents next to her own two sets of kindly, frail grandparents. And she put me next to the eccentric uncle who had systematically eaten his way through Manhattan. Meeting him was a highlight, and he was only too happy to share more details about his restaurant project, consuming his way from A to Z. I hit a question-asking stride.

"During those years, did you ever eat at home?"

"Not once. I didn't have time for that."

"Did you ever get food poisoning?"

"Never."

"What about the restaurants that closed down while you were still going down the list?"

He lit up at that one. "I kept my list strictly to the 1984 Yellow Pages. When a restaurant shut down, I'd just cross it off the list. But to maximize efficiency, I always called first to make sure they were open. It was all pre-Internet." As I think back on that conversation now, given what's happened to the restaurant business in the last two years alone, I'd put in single digits the percentage from that original list that survived.

There were a lot more questions I wanted to ask him, but the tinkling sound of silver against crystal, a high F-sharp, interrupted us.

Barb's two brothers, Rob and Danny (who had flown in from London with his family), gave a joint toast in the form of a stand-up routine, with inside jokes that had a lot of the room in stitches. Most of the jokes were at the expense of Barb's ex-boyfriends. Barb hadn't told me much about these guys, so I was riveted. They focused on the inferior looks of the exes, without being cruel. "Just when we were starting to wonder if our little sister needed to have her eyes checked, along came Ethan," said Robbie.

"And we're like, whoa! Sis, did you order this one straight from the Abercrombie & Fitch catalog?"

Then Brunch got up and took the mic. I was worried. Undiluted, Brunch was all jokester. I looked at Barb, who was standing a few feet away, and I could tell she was thinking what I was thinking: This could go badly. Brunch cleared his throat. "Hi, everyone. I'm Brendan, a.k.a. Brunch. I've known Ethan since my first day at Wharton." Now I sensed we were in for a ramble. He worked his way through my bio, or what he knew of it, starting with my job in tech support at Wharton Business School. He moved on to when he and Dave recruited me to write the software for Rita Receptionists, calling me the "Bill Shakespeare of computer programmers." That was nice. Barb looked at me and smiled.

"But just who was this guy? He talked so rarely that Dave and I thought he might be in witness protection." This got a big laugh. Brunch then proceeded to give a compendious recitation of my fits and starts with women. "Not a pretty picture. Ethan was our own George Costanza. The dorky clothes. Except Ethan's got hair to spare. Dave and I tried setting him up with a few women, but our attempts were a bust." True enough. I thanked Brunch silently for not saying anything more about that.

"He was a ship at sea. Then he found his anchor. Beautiful, sensible, caring Barb. They tried to keep their romance a secret at work, but we all noticed a new spring in Ethan's step. And then we noticed an electrical current running between his cubicle and hers. And now here we are. So here's to the anchor and her ship, no longer at sea. Barb and Ethan." And he raised his glass. I was touched, embarrassed, hating the attention, but inwardly pleased.

Then a familiar voice got my attention. "I'm Ethan's grandfather, Murray Steinhauer. Bernice and I are very happy to be here." He said how pleased he was that I was hitching my wagon to such a wonderful family. It was then that I noticed that he was holding his oboe. "Ethan, you might not know this, but when you were a baby, there was a piece written for the oboe that your mother loved." Now he was cradling the instrument in his hands. "She asked me to learn it so that I could play it for you. Whenever we visited Minneapolis, or when your parents brought you to Rochester, that's what I played for you. At bedtime. It's called 'Gabriel's Oboe.'" A few heads nodded in recognition. I drew a blank. I had never heard my grandfather mention the piece before. "I thought I'd dust it off after all these years. This is for you, Ethan and Barb. And for your mother. Sheila. She'd be very happy for you."

He lifted the instrument to his mouth and nervously slid the reed between his lips a few times. Then came a long A. Four measures in and the memory of the piece felt both immediate and impossible to place. He was wincing as he played, from the effort it took to send enough air from eighty-five-year-old lungs through those paper-thin reeds.

If music were words instead of sounds, I'd have heard the story of my mother's unfinished life in the notes he played. It was as if the melody had been kept safe all these years in my grandfather's oboe, and now it floated somewhere above us, in the liquid, lyrical movement of the notes. Seated next to me, Barb squeezed my hand. I was frozen. Now I remembered the piece completely. In those three minutes and thirty-five seconds, a series of sensations coursed through me like a flip-book. As my grandfather reached the end and hit an expectant E, I knew exactly what the final notes would be: a resolute D followed by the same note an octave above, shimmering and hopeful. I now remembered that when he played the piece to me at bedtime, I had come to expect those last two notes. But instead of moving on, he held the quiet unresolved E as one long stretched decrescendo. Then nothing.

What took the place of that last note wasn't silence, exactly, because no silence is pure. This silence was something more akin to room tone, that background hum unique to each space. There was the rustling sound of people shifting in their chairs, some murmuring. A few began to clap; many were wiping tears from their eyes—most of them, of course, knew the story of my childhood, more or less. My grandmother was dabbing her eyes with a tissue. As my grandfather took his seat, he retrieved his handkerchief from his breast pocket and wiped his brow.

I felt a tug at my hand. It was Barb, leading me to the dance floor, to the opening bars of Frank Sinatra and "Fly Me to the Moon," the song for our first dance. We had finished our jukebox project months earlier, and this had been the last song in the Seeburg Wall-O-Matic. Like countless grooms before me, I'd been dreading the first dance.

Without my knowing it (though I probably should have guessed), Barb had worked out a first-dance strategy with her parents. Realizing I would find it excruciating to be out there for the song's full two minutes and thirty-five seconds, Barb had asked her father, a suave dancer, to cut in halfway through. They executed the plan flawlessly. A little over a minute into the song (*"In other words, I love you . . ."*), Dan Pressman was tapping my shoulder. As father and daughter sailed away, Barb's mother materialized out of nowhere and hugged me. "We're so happy that you two found each other," she said into my ear. We stood side by side, watching them dance, Barb's white dress swirling around her legs like spun sugar each time her father led her into a turn.

7.

Soon after Barb and I got engaged, Rita Receptionists was sold to a big tech company. As Employee Number One, I was suddenly pretty well off, and Barb and I had plenty of cash to buy a house with. We loved our street in West Philadelphia, St. Marks Square, just west of the Penn campus. It was a short block of twelve identical row houses, all built in 1915, each with exactly 2,712 square feet of living space. Barb's apartment had once been part of one of those houses, which had been carved into three units. But most of the houses on the block were still single-family homes and seldom came on the market.

When we discovered there was one for sale three doors down, we bought it. It even had a linen closet on the second floor that was identical to the one in the apartment, and my first order of business was to fill the shelves with soft towels, leaving plenty of room for Mike the Cat. Our bathroom immediately grew redolent with the sweet scent of lavender, a smell I came to associate with Barb, who used a lavender soap that she ordered from an artisanal soap maker in New Mexico; this was one of her few self-indulgences. After we moved in, I'd see Barb and Mike the Cat and the one-eyed duck, all safely transferred to the new house, and let out a low long breath, a quiet declaration of contentment. Where the fireplace in Barb's apartment had long since been closed off, its twin in the new house was fully functioning; we stacked a cord of wood in the basement and built fires well into the spring. With four bedrooms, the house was far too big for the two of us. Barb didn't say it at the time, but I'm fairly certain that when we first looked at the house, she imagined a family.

PhD now in hand, Barb was busy applying for academic jobs in and around Philly. In the course of her research linking loneliness to physical illness, she and a couple of colleagues had published a stunning finding: loneliness can be as dangerous to your health as smoking a pack of cigarettes a day. Her work was so groundbreaking and, quite frankly, so extraordinary that I thought she'd have no trouble getting hired at one of the many schools near us.

Our wedding gift from Barb's parents was a weeklong honeymoon bike ride with Hill and Dale Adventures, in the destination of our choice. Dan and Bunny knew about my travel aversion, but they also believed that marriage would lead to a new and improved Ethan. Barb's parents weren't expecting to see me jettison my quirks necessarily ("They love you for all the reasons I do!" Barb insisted), but they hoped that marriage to their daughter would open me up a little to new ideas, such as a bike trip in a foreign country. Barb wanted to try the Piedmont region of northern Italy. She'd never been there (and neither, of course, had I). "It's where Barolos come from," she said, referring to her favorite red wine. "And it's where slow food got its start. Plus, truffles!"

Even if I had been up for the hassle of traveling to Europe, such a trip wouldn't have been my first choice for a honeymoon. I had to admit that the wine-and-food part sounded great. The bike part, on the other hand, sounded not just exhausting but, from the perspective of someone who used a bicycle strictly for transportation, a little pointless. All that pedaling, thirty miles a day, without really needing to get anywhere.

And I couldn't fathom the stress of riding a bike up and down unfamiliar roads, with Fiats whizzing past at a hundred miles an hour. And there was this: one in every three bike accidents results in a severe head injury, helmet or no. Then, of course, there was the problem of leaving Mike the Cat, whose purring had recently taken on an even more ominous tone. Just as worrisome was that he was no longer disappearing into the linen closet for his long cat naps. I surmised that he now lacked the strength to jump even as far as the first shelf, let alone his preferred perch on the third. Depositing him at Cat's Cradle was out of the question.

Looking back, I imagine all the things Barb could have called me, if she were inclined to tease: Captain Fearful. Horatio Homebody. Mister Worst-Case Scenario.

But she didn't; it was not her way. Instead, she listened patiently, then said, "Consider this your trial run at travel. You'll be surprised by how painless it is when you're traveling purely for pleasure."

I knew that she wanted the trip for all the right reasons, but it was also a test she was desperate for me to pass. I had to remind myself that Barb had grown up doing things like this. I told myself to trust her. I pictured myself in one of those workshops where participants pair up and practice falling into each other's arms. Of course I knew that Barb would catch me. But viscerally, well, there's only so much in one's emotional makeup—colored as it is by the past—that a person can control.

A few days after the wedding, we put Mike the Cat in the hands of Courtney the Cat Sitter and flew to Italy.

At a stop in London, we stood together at border control. The passport inspector looked for a free page on Barb's well-worn passport book to stamp, then turned to mine, which was pristine. A blank book. As was I.

During our layover at Heathrow, Barb knew exactly where to take me: the airport's Fortnum & Mason bar, which stood apart from everything else, an oasis amid the frenzy of duty-free shopping. We sat on blue-green velvet swivel stools and scrutinized menus of the same color. After a minute or two, I noticed that the same blue-green was the color of many things: the china, the tins of tea stacked on shelves, the linen.

The menu was another eye-opener. "I've never seen one with an entire caviar section," I told Barb.

"I know, right? And in an airport, no less," she said. She sat prim and straight, a plumb line from head to waist, her teal napkin folded with effortless elegance.

Barb ordered two "flat whites," espresso drinks that looked exactly like cappuccinos. "Flat whites are milkier," Barb explained.

On the flight to Turin, I looked out the window at a river snaking through the countryside, the same hue as everything at the Fortnum & Mason counter. Then without warning, the snow-capped Italian Alps appeared and soon stretched as far as I could see. Just as suddenly, as if I'd clicked on a new window on a computer screen, the mountains were gone, leaving me to wonder if I had imagined them. Now we were flying over land so flat and fertile I was put in mind of the Minnesota plains. Barb craned across my chest to see, and she squeezed my leg.

Hill and Dale Adventures had a reputation for pampering that proved to be well-earned; the company took care of everything. All we had to do was show up in the hotel lobby on the first morning of the ride. We were shuttled to a village on the outskirts of the city, where we were served lunch and introduced to our guides: an Italian, Luigi, and two Americans, Kevin and Sarah. The three guides, who looked to be barely out of college, were tanned, lean, and strong. They showed us our bikes, gave us a rundown on safety followed by navigation tips, and we were off.

From that moment, things took place in a kind of delicious slow motion. Every morning, our bikes stood waiting, the day's route slipped into map holders on the handlebars. Luigi, Kevin, and Sarah were reassuring sights each morning as they finished checking tire pressure and topping up water bottles. We filled sturdy plastic sandwich bags (why did everything in Europe seem so much more substantial?) with items from the snack table, which was covered with a checked tablecloth and laden with bowls of fruit, energy bars, and trail mix.

Barb quickly made friends with several in the group: Jan and Mike from Tacoma; Gwendolyn and Tom from Fort Lauderdale. And a dozen others. I have no clue how she did it, but she managed somehow to keep them all straight. She made friends with the guides too. Luigi and Sarah, she informed me, were a couple.

"How can you tell?" I asked.

"It's so obvious," she said. "Just watch their body language, the way they interact."

I started watching the two guides more closely. She was right. The two of them took note of each other in small but intimate

ways. During the "route rap" the next morning, the rundown of
the day's route, I could see they were tuned into each other, with
Luigi keeping his eyes on Sarah for an extra beat after saying or
handing something to her. "Good work, Detective," I said to
Barb that morning after setting off. "Were *we* that obvious?"

"Much more, I'm sure," she said.

With everyone invited to ride at their own pace, the riders
spread out quickly each morning, and within ten minutes Barb
and I found ourselves riding alone, the two of us in perfect sync.
Barb was a strong cyclist, taking the steep climbs in stride and
sailing down the long descents through sun-drenched countryside under a dazzling sky. With her just ahead of me, calling back
every so often—"Car up!" "Amazing view to the right!"—I felt
invincible. I was actually enjoying myself.

Whenever we came to a village—and we rode through many—
more often than not a church bell was ringing. I noticed them all
and made a point of giving Barb the musical note.

"That's an F-sharp!!" I would call out.

"How do you know that?!"

"I just do."

"Ethan Fawcett, you never cease to amaze me," she said, toss-
ing those words over her shoulder at me like flower petals, in a
tone reminiscent of her praise for her mother's peach cobbler.

Over the next couple of days, the notes from the church bells
started to really add up. After that first F-sharp came an E-flat,
then G, B-flat, D-flat, and E-flat again. After a while, I was
whistling made-up tunes using all the notes we heard, like Julie
Andrews and the do-re-mi song. Barb sang the notes back to me,
with lyrics composed of the Italian words she was picking up,

mostly to do with food and drink: *Carciofi. Vino rosso. Insalata mista. Cucina Piemontese.*

Looking back at that trip now, from a distance of four years and a lifetime, I know Barb and I must have ridden through Coazzolo, the sleepy little town where Izzy and I ducked into the church with the boys the day of the sudden rainstorm. And Barb and I might well have heard the church bell sounding the same mournful E-flat that Izzy and I noticed after we left the church. And of course we all must have wheeled straight through the village that's now a ghost town, and might even have seen Signora Fiore pulling her wagon across the empty square. But I have no memory of either place from my trip with Barb, nor can I recall any particulars of the many hamlets we rode through. Both Barb and I were content to let blur the town squares, the churches, the clotheslines stretching across streets, the village elders seated three and four to a bench, gesturing and speaking mile-a-minute Italian, just as we were content in 2018 to take for granted the prosaic day-in-and-day-out rhythm of those villages, as if it were something you could count on.

On the second afternoon of the trip, Barb got an email offering her a tenure-track position in the psychology department at Temple University. Barb was ecstatic and that night we treated everyone at our table to a celebratory glass of dessert wine.

While it's true that many specifics have faded, I can recall with utter reliability a general sense of well-being that I was still adjusting to, a kind of freedom I hadn't known before. That could have been what Barb meant when she said I needed experiences. She meant tangible experiences, yes, but she also meant experiences that were capable of lifting my heart and shifting it slightly before easing it back down into a different realm altogether. I spent the duration of that bike trip so joyous that I tilted toward giddiness. If Izzy had been a guide on that trip, what a different man she'd have seen! Then again, knowing Izzy, she was more likely to have seen straight through me, to the man Barb thought I was outgrowing, when what I was really doing was burying him in the shallowest of graves.

The fourth morning brought high drama. We stopped for the start of what the guides promised would be the two most exquisite nights of the trip. Our lodging was a seventeenth-century monastery built by Cistercian monks. Suspended high above a valley, the monastery had long since been sold and transformed into a five-star resort. Remarkably, despite the refinement that surrounded us, we could imagine the place as a monastery, protectively solid, with high walls and imposing entrances, the devotional aspect enhanced by its isolation.

At the start of the nineteenth century, the buildings and surrounding land had been bought by a rich Italian family, aristocrats named Contini. Vestiges of the Continis could be seen everywhere on the property. We felt like we were cohabiting with every period of the place's history. And now, in 2018, we were still surrounded on all sides by the architecture of prayer: outside our room, the "Ave Maria" chimed every morning (B-flat) from the old brick church on the grounds, and we ate our full luxurious breakfast in what was once the monks' refectory.

On the second morning at the monastery, when we gathered in the courtyard for the route rap, something seemed amiss. Our guides were there, but they weren't doing their usual thing with the bikes and the snacks and the water bottles. Instead, they were standing with two members of the hotel staff. Luigi was speaking in rapid-fire Italian and gesturing emphatically toward the cluster of bikes. Sarah was at his side, focused on his words. Kevin was going from bike to bike, tugging at the chains.

As other riders showed up, a buzz began to build, and within a few minutes, we were all in the know. Our eighteen bikes had been stored overnight under an awning behind the main building, in six lines, each three bikes deep. Someone had come along with a pair of wire cutters and severed the rear derailleur cable on the six bicycles in the front row. Just like that, six of our bikes were out of commission. Hill and Dale had been the victim of sabotage. The damaged bikes would need new cables, not something the guides kept on hand.

The guides were going to have to send for new bikes from the company's warehouse three hours away in Nice, and the replacements wouldn't arrive until late in the afternoon. This meant that six people would be sitting out the day's ride, one of them Barb.

The hotel staff was deeply apologetic and offered free spa treatments to the marooned guests, plus lunch on the house. I stayed behind in a show of solidarity with Barb, a gesture the other guests noted approvingly. Thanks to my new wife, pretty much everyone was aware that we were on our honeymoon.

Barb clearly appreciated my gallantry, but I could see she was unhappy. "I feel so violated," she told me. "I'm taking it personally."

"It was totally random." I tried to be reassuring. "They weren't singling people out. Maybe they don't like Hill and Dale. Or they detest Americans."

"Or they were taking a stand against the general notion of the leisure class," she said almost guiltily.

Jim, a ruddy-faced retiree from somewhere in Colorado who had taken a shine to Barb, didn't seem very put out, though he was among the victims. "This is a story we'll all be dining out on when we get home," he said. "The revenge of the Cable Guy!"

Jim was just the kind of lonely-looking person Barb tended to attract, and I began to worry that she would ask him to join us for the day. She might even see Jim as a question-asking opportunity: "Ethan, you could ask Jim about what he did before he retired." Or "Ethan, Jim told me he was a medic in Vietnam. You could ask him about that." Instead, she put her lips against my ear and whispered, "Let's go back to bed."

Our room, once a bare monk's cell and now appointed with the finest linens and bathroom fixtures, became a chamber of sybaritic excess. We left the blackout shutters wide open and daylight flooded the room. With Barb's face within a centimeter of mine I could see that the strong Italian sun had made her freckles so pronounced that the specks of white skin between them seemed the true discolorations. As we made love, our arousal heightened by the taboos of the cloistral surroundings, I silently thanked the bike saboteur.

We made it to the dining room five minutes before lunch service ended and, after a meal of *vitello tonnato* and *fonduta con tartufo*, we each had a massage, then went for a swim. Barb glided the length of the pool expertly, her body barely displacing the water as she propelled herself forward. When she turned her head to take a breath, the movement was perfectly timed with the arcing of her arm.

As we walked the frescoed halls and terracotta-tiled corridors, everyone we saw became a suspect in the Bike Caper—the groundskeeper, the pool attendant, the other guests roaming the property in the hotel's long cowled robes, each with pockets deep enough to stash a cutting tool. As we passed one robed couple, both staring blankly in what I assumed was a massage-induced trance, I said to Barb, "Maybe the bike cutter was one of those monk ghosts."

Barb smiled slyly. "What does Columbo think?"

I dipped straight into my best Columbo slouch and rubbed my chin.

"Ma'am, that's an awfully good question."

She sighed. "We'll probably never know who it was. Even if the hotel eventually figures it out, we'll be long gone."

Before dinner, we took our cocktails into one of the parlors, where a chess board was set up, the pieces made of intricately carved alabaster. Barb took forever to move, cradling her face in her hands as she pondered the board for minutes on end. As soon as she picked up a piece to move it, she looked up at me, waiting for me to shake my head.

"That's going to result in a pretty quick checkmate," I said.

"How?"

I zipped through five moves, knocking out a pawn, a bishop, and a rook before cornering her undefended king.

"Oh," she said as she watched me put the pieces back. As soon as she started looking at the board again, I stared at her, doubting I could ever tire of taking her in.

The next morning, we were back on our bikes, the cable-cutting incident all but forgotten. And by the end of those magical seven days, my mood was carefree, bordering on madcap.

So perhaps it was the desire to recapture that feeling that compelled me, four years and three months later, minus one wife but plus two sons, the world a changed place, to try to replicate the trip. Looking back, it seems clear that I was setting myself up for disaster. Then again, sometimes you understand these things only after they've happened. I could say I wanted Tommy and Sam to experience what Barb and I had experienced, that I wanted to give them a glimpse of their fuddy-duddy dad in a completely different context. I now realize my conceit—that by repeating that magical route, I might not merely stop time but force it into reverse.

8.

IN RETROSPECT, OF COURSE, I SHOULD HAVE CONFESSED TO Barb early on that the prospect of having children petrified me. Earlier than I did, that is, which was after the bike trip. It came up on the flight home. There was a crying baby on the plane a few rows behind us. The baby was miserable all the way from London to Philly, and I felt terrible for the parents, who also had a toddler with them.

During the descent, the baby started screaming its head off, a piercing, inconsolable cry.

"That baby must be congested," Barb said.

"Congested?"

"All that sinus pressure," she said, and she launched into a gruesome description of what she believed was causing the baby so much pain—an obstructed sinus and the changing pressure inside the aircraft, resulting in an excruciating "squeeze effect." As a prop, she pulled the half-full plastic Evian bottle from my seat pocket. It looked like it had been run over by a car.

"That's what's happening inside the baby's head," Barb said. For effect, as the plane continued its descent, Barb unscrewed the top of the water bottle and the sides instantly popped back out again.

This airplane headache sounded so horrific that I envisioned the autopsy of a brain after a congested descent ending up as an exhibit at the Mütter Museum. "I've had it happen," Barb said. "The pain went straight into my molars." I was amazed that anyone who'd had a headache like that would ever step foot on a plane again.

I'd had more than enough of the topic, but Barb was on a roll. "Our kids," she said. "One sniffle before a flight and they're getting a decongestant."

It was the first time she had ever said "our kids"—and, believe me, I'd been listening for it for months. In fact, I promised myself that as soon as Barb used that phrase, we would have a conversation. I'd been dreading this moment, and here it was.

Wisely, I didn't counter her wish to be a parent with my meticulously researched arguments against bringing children into a world in which they would be forced to traverse a minefield of hazards—and now, for the record, you could add airplane descents to the list. Now more than ever, it seems unnecessarily cruel to add more souls to this bellicose and increasingly scorched earth of ours. Instead, I mumbled something about how unfit I would be as a parent.

Barb looked at me sideways. "Unfit? Are you crazy?"

I said nothing.

"You're serious," she said. But she would have none of it. "Ethan, look at all the people who do it. Billions and billions. And you'll be a better dad than ninety-nine percent of them!"

Those words, more than anything she might have said, snapped my heart in two. Because only I knew beyond a doubt how ill-equipped I was to be the guardian of another living soul. Luckily, amid the hubbub of disembarking from the plane, the subject was dropped.

When we arrived home, we were greeted by Courtney the Cat Sitter, who informed us that Mike the Cat was at the vet. She hadn't wanted to worry us while we were away, and by the time she'd taken him to the vet, we were on the plane. She said he was growing increasingly "phlegmatic." Courtney, who was an English major at Temple, was one of those fancy-word people. She could have just said "low energy" and we would have gotten the picture.

"They're going to run some tests," Courtney said. We started asking her questions, but she already had her backpack on and her answers were curt. When did he start to show signs of illness? ("Thursday.") Was he eating? ("Not really.") Did the vet call to say what the tests showed? ("No.") Had he been drinking water? This one inspired a lengthier response. "It's been inordinately hot here over the past few days. He might have been dehydrated. But it's possible that his curtailed fluid intake was a sequela of something other than the heat." Now she was a medical student? "Is that what the vet told you?"

"Essentially, yes. Well, maybe."

I wrote her a check, adding the fifteen dollars she had spent on cab fare to the vet. As I spelled her name out, a voice kept popping into my head, saying, *If only you had been here, this wouldn't have happened.*

Although drunk with jet lag, we got in the car and drove straight to the vet, arriving just as they were closing. The door was locked, but we must have looked pitiful, because the front-office assistant let us in. One of the vets was still there. The assistant led us into an exam room, disappeared briefly, and then reappeared with Mike the Cat and deposited him into Barb's lap. "Dr. Crew will be right in," she said.

Mike the Cat looked terrible, a shadow of the feline we had left in Courtney's care ten days earlier. I couldn't tell whether he had really deteriorated that much while we were gone or if the decline had been gradual all along and was visible to us only now, after we'd been away.

It turned out to be the latter. Dr. Crew, a dapper man in a bow tie who looked to be in his late fifties, came in, said hello to us briefly, and immediately began petting Mike the Cat. "I'm not the doctor who saw him this morning, so this fine fellow is new to me." He was running his hand along Mike the Cat's crenellated spine. I appreciated the hail-fellow-well-met formality, but it was awfully incongruous, as Mike the Cat didn't look at all fine.

Barb was rubbing the base of Mike the Cat's left ear and I was bent over the two of them, rubbing the right ear. His breaths were shallow and rapid. He was purring, but there was a rattle along with it. I confessed quietly to Barb that I had been hearing that rattle-like purr on and off for a couple of months. She said she'd heard the same.

"What would you recommend?" Barb asked Dr. Crew.

He looked up at her, then looked at Mike the Cat's chart. "Well, the blood work came back and there's nothing obvious. Nothing on the physical exam either. No tumors, and his temperature is normal. He could just be pooped out. Eighteen years is a good long life for a cat."

Barb and I were quiet, so the vet continued. "It's a pretty safe bet that his quality of life isn't likely to improve," he said. "You can take him home. Or we can give him an injection now that would let him drift off peacefully."

This was a speech he delivered all the time, but it was the first time I was hearing it. End things then and there? Really? Barb must have seen the shock register on my face. "We just got back from a trip and haven't been able to spend time with him," she told the doctor. "As long as we're not prolonging any suffering, I think we'd like to take him home." I was grateful to her for stepping up with that plan.

Mike the Cat was so limp that we didn't even have to put him in his cat carrier for the car ride home. Ordinarily, he'd have been meowing and terrified in the car. But now he didn't have enough energy to freak out. He lay on Barb's lap while I drove. Barb was petting him gently and reminiscing with him about their years together, starting with when she'd brought him home from the Humane Society as a kitten to all his happy years on Railroad Avenue in Haverford, where he'd had free rein outside, followed by her four years away at college, then his most recent stint in Philly, when he'd had to adjust to life as an indoor cat, and finally the addition of me into their life.

"I really love him," she said to me. "And I know you do too." She moved her hand from Mike the Cat's back to my knee and rested it there.

We pulled into our driveway, and as soon as I shut off the engine I realized I was crying—not just a couple of tears; I must have been sobbing because my nose was dripping onto my pants. I wiped it with my arm. When would it stop? How could I make it stop? How could I stanch this flow of despair? My head was bent and I saw Barb's hand reach for the glove compartment and open it slowly. She produced a packet of tissues, took one out, and handed it to me as she stroked my leg. I had cried so few times in my life (in fact, I had no memory of crying before that) I suppose I didn't know that tears can stop as spontaneously as they start, which is exactly what happened. From start to finish, my tears might have lasted all of thirty seconds, though while it was going on it felt like a lifetime. Neither of us made a move to get out of the car.

Barb spoke in a near whisper, yet her words filled the car. "Pets," she said. "We really get attached to them."

More quiet. Then, in that same hushed tone, her voice a salve all its own, Barb told me she had a film-studies professor in college who was a screenwriter in Hollywood and was commissioned to write one of the Lassie movies.

"He wrote a scene where Lassie gets washed over a waterfall," she said. "The studio executive threw the script across the room, going, 'Oh my God, he killed the dog!'"

"He killed Lassie?" I asked.

"No!" she said. "He didn't kill Lassie. He just wanted to take the dog out of the movie for a few scenes because he was so sick of writing dog directions. 'Tail wag. Head tilt. Raised paw. Bark. Whimper.' He said it was just so boring."

"So Lassie survives the waterfall?" I asked hopefully.

"Of course!" Barb said. "Then magically reappears in the climax of the movie to rescue Timmy."

It felt good to change the subject. "We should watch a Lassie movie sometime."

"Definitely," she said.

We went upstairs and fell asleep on top of the bed with our clothes on, the cat between us. We woke up at 4:00 a.m., when we'd be up in Italy anyway, and I carried Mike the Cat downstairs. There was no more purring. Even the rattly sound was gone. His breathing was labored, and he hardly moved. Barb made coffee, and we sat at the kitchen table. As soon as the vet opened at 8:00 a.m., we drove there. A different vet this time, a young woman with a gentle manner, administered the injection.

If anything were to convince me once and for all never to have kids, these last hours with Mike the Cat should have done it. But—and I cannot tell you why—the effect was precisely the opposite.

9.

ONCE I CONSENTED TO HAVING KIDS, I WAS GIDDY WITH anticipation. I kept the refrigerator stocked with fresh whole milk and urged Barb to drink a glass with every meal, figuring that if her bones were healthy she'd be more likely to have a baby with healthy, cooperative bones, instead of bones gone haywire like poor Harry Eastlack.

I still possessed the copy of Dr. Spock's book that I'd found in my grandparents' attic years earlier.

My grandparents died within a year of each other. My grandmother went first, soon after Barb and I married, of a cruel, quick cancer. She was followed by my heartbroken grandfather, who died after a massive stroke. My grandparents' lawyer wrote to say they'd left half their estate to me and the rest to the Rochester Symphony. I asked the lawyer to give most of my half to the symphony as well, to support the orchestra's principal oboist, who became the Murray and Bernice Steinhauer Principal Oboe.

They also left the contents of their house to me. I instructed the lawyer to donate everything to Goodwill, with the exception of the items from my mother's room—then and forever my mother's room. When a UPS truck pulled up a couple of weeks later, I was disappointed to see that the driver had just two boxes to deliver, neither very large. At some point, my grandparents must have cleared out the room. The boxes held just a few books (including several of the ones I'd read) and a few other random items. The baton was gone, as was my baseball bat. But my mother's high school yearbook had survived. One item I pulled from the box was a brown cardigan with big leather buttons—my grandfather's wintertime clothing staple. How that sweater ended up mixed in with my mother's possessions I'll never know. But I was glad to have it.

The Dr. Spock volume had traveled with me through life. In fact, I'd pretty much memorized the parts of the book with my grandmother's notes and came to believe that therein lay all truth about raising children. One night after dinner, I presented the book to Barb, enclosed in gift wrap covered with shiny baby giraffes.

She unwrapped it slowly, taking care not to rip the paper.

"Benjamin Spock?" she asked. Seeing that book in my wife's hands, read a hundred times over, was a little startling, and I felt myself catching my breath. She stroked the jacket with the palm of her hand, then opened the book to the inscription in the front: "To Murray and Bernice, the very fortunate new parents of Miss Sheila Steinhauer. You know more than you think you do!" She looked up at me, confused. Of course she knew about the famous Dr. Spock, who'd worked as both pediatrician and psychiatrist, but I'd never told her of his connection to my family.

"My grandparents bought their house from him," I said. "It's the house my mother grew up in."

"Really?" This bit of news clearly impressed her.

I had told Barb my mother's maiden name, but this was the first time she'd seen it written. "Sheila Steinhauer," she murmured, almost to herself. She started leafing through the book, stopping to read aloud some of the pearls of wisdom my grandmother had underlined. "Don't be afraid to trust your own common sense." "Young infants can't anticipate the future; they live entirely in the here and now."

Barb was especially amused by Dr. Spock's primer on toilet training: Toddlers don't really understand why they should sit on the potty instead of just filling up their diapers. They typically find their bodily productions interesting, not disgusting. They don't see what all the fuss is about if the contents of their diaper get smeared around a bit.

When it came to conceiving a child, Barb believed time was of the essence, having read a few articles that mentioned it could take several tries once you start. I was more than happy to take our time, because every month that we failed to conceive gave me more time to prepare the house. Countless hazards lay in wait for our children, but I figured that if I made a few pre-emptive fixes, I could keep some of those threats at bay.

"I think there's something wrong with our hot water," Barb said one day after getting out of the shower. "It's not getting hot enough."

"I reset the heater down to 110 degrees," I told her.

"What? Why?"

"It was set at 145 degrees, which can produce a full-thickness burn in less than two seconds," I explained. "Did you know that half of all scald burns are serious enough to require skin grafts?" She was looking at me with a blank stare. Then she spoke.

"Ethan, first of all, it's going to take at least nine months for a baby to arrive. Do you see a baby in this room? There's no baby. And even if there were a baby in a crib right over there," she pointed to a spot next to our bed, "newborns don't climb into bathtubs and turn the hot water handle. So could I *please* have my hot water back?"

That small setback notwithstanding, within a few weeks I had the house pretty well babyproofed. All the outlets got covered and breakables put away. I also locked away our tablecloths and placemats (too easily pulled off a table). Then I ditched all the potential poisons.

"What happened to all my little perfumes?" Barb asked, referring to a collection of tiny crystal bottles filled with *eau de* this and that she had arranged on the bedroom dresser.

"I put them on the top shelf in the medicine cabinet," I said. She was regarding me as if we were meeting for the first time. Her silence prompted me to explain. "Barb, there are two million calls a year to poison-control centers."

"Okay, fine," she huffed, and she pivoted to leave the bedroom.

"Better safe than sorry, right?" I said, though I was speaking to the back of her head.

When Barb was ovulating, we had sex at least once a day, and I can tell you there's nothing quite like sex with a goal. One of Barb's friends told her that once you start trying, it saps the joy out of sex and makes it feel like work. But that isn't what happened to us. Every time we made love it felt like a win-win. At least for the first six months. Then Barb started to worry.

"I'm almost thirty," she lamented. I was closing in on thirty-five, which was also starting to feel ancient.

Every month when she got her period she delivered the news in a hangdog tone.   ·

"It will happen eventually," I tried to reassure her.

"But I don't want eventually," she said. "I want now!"

At the one-year mark, we went to a fertility clinic for tests. Barb's tests came back completely normal, all reproductive parts in fine working order. The problem lay with me. Somewhere along the line my body had stopped producing sperm. Or maybe it had never produced sperm in the first place. The medical condition, we were told, was called *azoospermia*, and mine was of a variety that couldn't be treated.

Instead of devastation, suddenly finding out I was sterile gave rise to something akin to redemption. Some higher order was confirming what I'd suspected all along: I was not meant to be a father. I felt the euphoria of the damned.

Barb was so busy worrying about me that I wasn't sure how she felt upon learning that she had hitched her wagon to a reproductive dud. When I asked her, she said, "Well, I'd prefer to have a little Ethan, with that big brain of yours and all that quiet energy. But that might not be in the cards. And it doesn't matter. I know you'll be a great dad whether you're the biological parent or not."

We came up with plan B: a sperm donor and artificial insemination. While browsing the leading sperm bank's website, we were amused to discover a catalog filled with photographs, physical descriptions, personal essays, and medical histories.

"Oh, what a cute kid!" Barb said. She was looking at Donor 15798. The photo of each prospect showed the donor as a child, with a cute caption. Donor 15798's caption was "The Force Is with Him," and his photo showed a grinning six- or seven-year-old, down on one knee, a football tucked under his arm. His front teeth were missing.

"Where are his teeth?" I asked.

"All kids lose their baby teeth. He just didn't have his permanent teeth yet," she said. "But you know that. You're just being difficult."

"Look at his answer to this." I pointed to the question "What is the one thing everyone should know about you?"

"'I love string lights,'" Barb read aloud. "Okay, you're right," she said, her voice tinged with disappointment in The Force Is with Him.

As she hovered over the description of the next prospect, Donor 14854 ("Life of the Party"), I realized I was thinking what I feared she was thinking: Maybe it would be better if the person we chose were completely different from me. Life of the Party, if true to his handle, could be just the guy. Still, I couldn't help but point out an obvious shortcoming. "Life of the Party doesn't seem very literate," I said.

"He majored in philosophy!" she countered.

"Okay, but under 'favorite foods' he put 'healthy tasty stuff.'"

Barb came to Life of the Party's defense. "He doesn't claim to be a writer." I felt a twinge of jealousy—was I now competing with LotP for Barb's affection?

"Six one. That's a good height," she added. That stung. I'm five nine.

Before we could see beyond the picture of a ruddy-cheeked kid, up popped a window: "Low Vial Alert! Final Inventory for this Donor."

"He must be popular," she said.

"Look," I pointed out. "His favorite animal is a dachshund. They're ridiculous dogs." An eminently sensible observation on my part, but Barb didn't appreciate it.

"Lots of people love dachshunds," she said.

She called up Life of the Party's personal essay. "What are you most proud of and why?" it asked. His answer: "I am the proudest of the success my mom has had with the school she started."

"That's so sweet," Barb said. "And his mom started a school, just like my mom." She was really stuck on Life of the Party, whose sperm was flying off the shelf.

"But it's about his mom, not him," I said. "Why isn't he proud of anything about himself? Is he living his dream or his mother's dream?"

Under staff comments, a sperm bank employee wrote, "He is the person to go to if you're looking for a good vegan restaurant." "That could be code for New Age Dolt," I pointed out. "Look. His favorite poem is 'Charge of the Goddess.' By Starhawk."

"Ugh," she said in apparent agreement.

"What's the business model of this place?" I asked.

"What do you mean?"

"I mean, do the donors get paid just for donating sperm, or per vial they produce? Or do they get a royalty fee every time a vial of their sperm gets bought? You know. Sperm residuals. If they get a royalty they might be tempted to pad their résumés to move sperm."

Truth be told, I really wasn't liking the look of any of these guys. I was actually feeling a little inferior, not sure what my tagline would be and whether my sperm (if I actually had any) would move on the open market.

"This one's a medical student," Barb said, having finally—to my great relief—abandoned Life of the Party. Now she was studying photos of Donor 15021, "Brilliant Bookworm."

"Nope," I said. "It says he's premed, which is completely different. Do you know how many people start college as premed and flame out as soon as they take organic chemistry?"

"Ethan, he looks a little like you." She was looking at a few photos of Brilliant Bookworm as an adolescent, who was already wearing glasses. "His eyesight could be a problem," I said, pushing my own glasses up on the bridge of my nose.

"Look at his adorable button nose," she said cheerily.

"You have to think about how a nose like that would age," I said. "It can be cute when you're a kid but really wrong on an adult face."

"There's a way to know," Barb said. She was on Brilliant Bookworm's "facial features" page. Nose shape: "straight." Nose width: "wide." She had me with that one.

"He's Catholic," I said.

"What's wrong with that? You're half Catholic!" Then she laughed. "Religion isn't genetic, Ethan." Barb was really liking this guy. "His special skill is chess, like yours," she said. "And he's fair-skinned. A ginger like me."

"That's high risk for skin cancer, times two."

Now she was exasperated. "Why are you rejecting everything, every single permutation? Everybody's got some fatal flaw."

"I'm just not sure a sperm donor is the way to go. It feels like such a crapshoot."

"I don't think it's any more of a crapshoot than having kids from your own sperm. You never know what's lurking in your genes that just didn't get expressed."

"Okay," I said. "But do you really want to take the chance that your kid shares genes with someone whose favorite writer is named Skyhawk?"

"Starhawk," she corrected me.

She flipped down the lid to her laptop. "Maybe we should just adopt."

I was getting emotional whiplash. No sooner had I gotten used to the idea of having kids than I found out I couldn't produce my own. And the minute I'd absorbed the decree that I was not destined to procreate, we were staring at pictures of strangers. And now adoption?

Barb pointed out that I was turning into a cliché of a man set on propagating his genes, of thinking no child would be acceptable unless that child shared my DNA. Little did she know that wasn't what this was about, that I was really worried that any adoption agency that wasn't asleep at the switch would see through me, catching on immediately to my inability to keep another human safe. But I couldn't tell Barb that. Instead, I said we should keep talking about it, but adoption sounded okay.

Within a few weeks, Barb found Tommy and Sam.

10.

WITH FRESH INFUSIONS OF CAPITAL FROM OUR NEW CORPORATE owners, by late 2019 Rita Receptionists was growing apace. I was away on a company retreat in the Poconos, where cell service was nonexistent. With my phone out of commission for two days, I had no clue what was going on back in Philly.

When I got home, Barb greeted me at the door. I knew right away that something was up because she never did that. "I have a surprise for you." Beaming, she took my hand and led me into the living room. "Ethan, meet Tommy and Sam."

There on the sofa sat the twins, pale and fine-boned and undernourished, their mouths as red and full as cherries. They both wore overalls that were clean but faded. Sam's were rolled up to the middle of his calves. The sleeves of his blue cotton shirt were also rolled up, with great precision in each fold. Tommy, on the other hand, had on an oversized short-sleeved shirt beneath his overalls. The sleeves billowed around his reed-thin arms. He was wearing a plain blue baseball cap cocked to one side, Sam a wide-brimmed straw hat tilted back on his head. Both boys were barefoot. They were seated within an inch of each other.

I was stunned. "This might be too much to get my mind around," I said.

Barb persisted. "Listen, I know this seems crazy, but let me explain. This'll give us a chance to try our hand at parenting, at least for now." Her eyes were beseeching.

Tommy and Sam were eight or nine years old. They appeared to be identical twins, but they could have been fraternal twins who happened to look an awful lot like each other.

"Frank called while you were gone. These two were adopted from Russia, but the family didn't work out and someone needs to take them on a temporary basis," she said, grinning.

"Russia?" I was skeptical. "Isn't there a ban against Americans adopting Russian kids?"

"They came just before it went into effect."

Barb could see that I wasn't going along with any of this just yet, and she grew slightly exasperated. "Ethan, work with me here."

This was Barb through and through. It was just like her to be moved deeply by kids suffering from abuse or neglect. And orphans to boot! How could I possibly say no to such benevolence? Nor could I find anything to object to when it came to them: Tommy appeared to be a look-you-straight-in-the-eyes kind of boy, and Sam was the shy one, peering tentatively from under his wide-brimmed hat. They looked like throwbacks to an earlier era.

Her imploring finally won me over. "Sure," I said. "Why not? Practice is always a good thing."

Then I thought of something. "My father would really like these guys," I said. I thought of the way my dad looked at the discarded objects he found on the street and saw their full potential. Some family had given up on these boys. I suddenly had the urge to keep them safe and bring out all they could be.

"Right," she agreed. "Russians have such creative souls."

The boys' English was almost nonexistent. At first, we communicated with them using mainly hand signals and props. I bought flashcards with pictures of the objects I was referring to: toilet; jacket; bed; water.

"It's definitely hard to get their attention," Barb said one morning when she came into the living room to find both boys on the couch. They didn't turn their heads when she said good morning. "Maybe they're both deaf."

She had a point. Nothing seemed to startle them. To help us with their backstory, I did a little reading up on Russian orphanages. In those brutal places, where not one iota of nurturing can be found, children develop an alarming level of detachment; they grow conditioned not to cry because no one came when they did. After a few years in such a place, lord only knew the magnitude of distrust a child must internalize when it came to grown-ups, people who should make you feel protected and cared for but did not. Maybe they thought that Barb and I were just another pair of adults entering their lives who were bound to disappoint, like all the others.

I was also reading about the complex, private language twins sometimes invent, a phenomenon called *idioglossia*. The boys didn't speak to us, but they clearly had a way of understanding each other; they just didn't want to let us in on it yet. I told Barb I didn't think they were deaf. I thought they were coping. Who could blame them for retreating into their pas de deux, a dance they performed only with and for each other?

"That makes sense," Barb said when I offered my analysis. "See, Ethan? I told you you'd be a great parent." Her words made me flush with quiet pride.

Since the boys were already well past toddlerhood when they arrived, an entire category of potential accidents could be stricken from the list. Barb got her little perfume bottles back. Like most children who have been in institutions, Tommy and Sam displayed a level of lassitude, which might have been cause for concern, but I saw it as a bonus. They were not prone to out-of-control behavior of any kind. And they definitely weren't the type of boys to tear around on skateboards. All told, from the day Barb brought them home, I considered us incredibly lucky.

Our house was big enough that each boy could have had a room of his own, but I thought it made more sense to keep them together. Twins are strongly attached to each other because they shared a womb, and identical twins are even more so because at one point they were literally the same person. Separating them now might be traumatic. This seemed especially important at night. I worried that all the effort required for them to tamp down their adrenaline could give rise to nightmares. If they had each other close by, it would have a calming effect. The plan worked. I never heard a peep from their room.

I'm no language teacher, but it occurred to me that watching American TV might be a good way for the boys to absorb everyday English. We didn't own a TV, so I bought one and signed us up for premium cable service, with channels to spare. I introduced the boys to all my old favorites: *Sesame Street* for some basics and *Mister Rogers' Neighborhood* for homespun wisdom. Sam—such a sweet, gentle soul—came to life when *Mister Rogers* was on. It dawned on me that my grandfather's cardigan looked a lot like Fred Rogers's sweater, so when *Mister Rogers* was on I let Sam wear it. I added *Jeopardy!* to the list of TV shows, to help them build their overall knowledge. And, of course, *Columbo*. By the time Columbo arrives on the scene, the crime has already occurred, making the show almost all talk, with blessedly little grisly action. I hoped it would help the boys not just with their language skills, but also with logic and deduction. Sometimes I'd come into the living room and Barb and the boys would be watching one of the shows without me. "Mister Rogers is such a great guy," Barb said on one of these occasions, sighing. "I thought I'd grown out of it, but I guess not. I forgot how much I like watching TV."

"I'm so sorry to interrupt you, Ma'am, but are you the lady of the house, by any chance?" I asked in my most deferential Columbo voice. Barb laughed. The new demands on our life were keeping us from having much time alone, so it was a thrill to see her light up, a reminder of a more carefree time. "Why, yes I am, Lieutenant."

"According to my watch, it's eight p.m., but this watch . . . I've been having a hard time with it lately. I'm not sure I trust it." I held the watch up to my ear and tapped it conspicuously. "Ma'am, do you happen to have the correct time?"

"It's eight thirty-five," Barb said.

"Yep. That's what I thought. This darn watch." I shook my head and tapped the watch again. "So that leads me to think it's time for bed for these two young men." I scooped up the boys— they were as light as balsa—and tucked one under each arm so they were practically horizontal and carried them off to their room. They squirmed a little but seemed content. Behind me, I heard Barb chuckling to herself.

Barb was careful not to say anything snide ("You've really fallen into the butter now, Mr. Recluse," for example), and definitely nothing inappropriate, about the situation we found ourselves in a few months after Tommy and Sam arrived. It was early 2020, and the world had taken too tragic a turn for that. On the inhospitable orb billions of people now discovered Earth to be, this much was clear: When Rita Receptionists went 100 percent virtual, I was vindicated. For years I'd been saying there was no need for our receptionists, who were virtual by definition, to go into an office in order to pretend they were in an office. Now, with a global pestilence suddenly upon us, there was no pretending, since everyone on the planet who had the luxury to do so was staying home. I was wired for quarantine, but I worried about my wife, whose social-butterfly streak wasn't likely to take well to staying under a single roof.

I set myself up in a nook off the living room, so that I could keep an eye on the boys. I brought Strip the Furby home and placed him next to my computer. When Barb passed my work area, she'd pat his head and say little things like, "Hey, Strippy," or "Having a good day, Strip?"

All that American TV notwithstanding, the boys were picking up English more slowly than I had hoped. So in a gesture of reciprocity, I decided to learn some Russian. I thought I'd go for just the basics: *Yes. No. Maybe. That's good. Are you hungry? Are you tired? Do you want X, Y, or Z?* I put a translation app on my phone that let me speak an English word into the phone and out came Russian. It wasn't so different from reverse engineering. When the boys heard the translation on the phone, they tuned in. After a few days of this, it was clear that our translation game was a way for us to bond. For one thing, I could make myself instantly understood. For another, hearing their native tongue appeared to soothe both the boys, especially when delivered in the sweet, lilting tones of the Siri-like Russian woman inside the phone.

I decided to read aloud to the boys. Instead of grade school pablum, I took a bold step and chose *Anna Karenina*. My mother's old Modern Library edition with the red cover was one of the books that had arrived from Minnesota after my grandfather's death. Though I couldn't read to them in Russian, I could read to them *about* Russia, which I thought might help maintain a connection to their native country. If they needed a word translated, I could simply tap the microphone icon on my translation app.

"Have you read this?" Barb asked me when she saw the book on the boys' nightstand.

"A long time ago," I said. I was seated at the foot of Tommy's bed, ready to start part one, chapter one.

"In college?"

I shook my head.

"Who reads *Anna Karenina* voluntarily? I mean, what guy reads *Anna Karenina* voluntarily?"

She really wanted to know. So I told her about finding the book on my mother's bookshelf. And how when I was fourteen, over the course of an especially long and brutal Minnesota winter, I'd read *Anna Karenina* straight through, with no way of knowing at the time what an eerie coincidence it would be to have Tommy and Sam—with their particular heritage—enter my life so many years later.

"Did you like it?" she asked, biting her lower lip expectantly.

I nodded. "A lot."

"So did I," she said. "But I never could put my finger on Vronsky. Everyone else, I felt like I had their number. But Vronsky? What a puzzle, right?" Barb was looking at Tommy and Sam. "Even if it's lost on these two," she said, "I'm really looking forward to hearing you read this." She dragged a small armchair across the room and settled herself in. I put on a different voice for each character. Anna was a little husky, her lover Vronsky a bass, Kitty melodious, and her sister Dolly a tad pinched, with a mild case of vocal fry. Alexei Alexandrovich, Anna's aggrieved husband, got a big and pompous tone at first, then a whiny, self-pitying one. Levin, Kitty's husband, in chronic existential crisis, had bugged me the first time around, so I gave him a reedy sound and threw in some interpretive license by adding a touch of modern upspeak at the end of his lines. Accounting for a half dozen translation interruptions per page, I estimated that if I averaged two pages a night, it would take me roughly fourteen months to read the entire book. At the time, I thought I was reading that book aloud for the boys' benefit, and it might well have started out that way, but now I know I did it for Barb.

Tommy and Sam listened as I read but said little, sometimes cooing softly at each other in their private gibberish. Barb didn't really seem concerned, and I knew they would speak to us when they were good and ready.

We'd been talking about getting another cat, to take the place of Mike the Cat. We both missed him. Barb was particularly enthusiastic and was online every day perusing the lists from local shelters, which were running low on cats up for adoption, as everyone in Philly now wanted a new pet. (Dogs were a bit more popular, since they served the dual role as companion and excuse to go outside.) Barb put us on a few waiting lists.

She made a point of taking a long walk every morning, return-ing with a waxed white bakery bag containing a single and very welcome maple-glazed. But one morning a few weeks into the shutdown, she came home to tell me, mournfully, that our local Happy Donut had closed. I didn't want to show my disappoint-ment because Barb seemed so upset about it, so I told her I was okay with it, that eating sugary donuts wasn't a behavior I should be modeling for the boys. But I was quietly crushed.

I came to dread the idea of leaving the house, but Barb forced the issue when she told me one night that she was craving beef with oyster sauce. It was one of the few dishes I knew how to make, and she loved it. We were stocked up on many things, including oyster sauce, but we didn't have the perishable ingre-dients on hand.

"Why don't you go to the store in the morning for mushrooms and bok choy," she suggested. "Do you mind?"

How could I say no? Barb was doing all the shopping. "Sure," I said. "I'll go first thing tomorrow."

If she sensed my uneasiness, she didn't show it. After we went to bed, as Barb lay next to me, dreaming about the stir-fried beef in her future, I was fretting about my shopping trip. To calm myself, I tried some deep breathing and mapped out a strategy in my head. I'd tape the grocery list to the back of one of my nitrile gloves. I'd get to the store by 7:50 a.m., ten minutes before it opened, to get a good place in line. I'd buy not just the ingredi-ents for the stir fry, but flowers for Barb and a few other things she would never get for herself, like expensive cheeses.

Nothing went as planned. I was in the car by 7:15 a.m., but by the time I got to the store, shoppers were already standing on their strips of blue tape spaced six feet apart. My mask fogged my glasses. Then a store employee came out and announced, "Anyone under sixty, please wait in line across the parking lot."

The other line, already formed, was even longer. Still, I waited. One man who stood a few strips ahead of me had a winter scarf looped across his face. Did that count as a mask? By the time I had been handed a cart and was inside, it was 9:27.

We entered at the produce section, which was roped off from the rest of the store. Arrows designated how we were to zigzag our way through the fruits and vegetables, which were, amazingly enough, fresh and bountiful. I thought I'd see something like 1980s Prague, where lines to buy mealy apples spanned for blocks. But this was a horn of plenty. There were half a dozen types of mushrooms to choose from, and I worked quickly, feeling pressure to keep moving. I could barely see out of my steamed-up glasses and fought an urge to remove my mask. After filling a bag with criminis, I headed for the bok choy. But things had bogged down. Someone was taking his sweet time. It was the guy with the scarf, who was now the guy without the scarf, the makeshift piece of protective gear having fallen away from his face. As if ordained to thwart my plan, he was standing over the bok choy, methodically placing bunch after bunch into individual plastic bags. Admittedly, it looked like a beautiful stack of bok choy, and no one could blame him for being drawn to it. But why was he so slow? Why was he taking so much of it? And why was there no employee rushing to the scene to address the mask violation? The bags were tough to open, so he was licking a finger to separate the plastic. I winced—the place was feeling like a viral hothouse.

Some people were walking around Mr. No Scarf. Others were waiting, their impatience palpable. A posted sign warned of "No Reentry" into the produce section after leaving. I desperately wanted the bok choy, but with this guy leaning over it—not to mention the broccoli, cauliflower, and other bok choy–proximate vegetables—I faced a binary choice. Wait or don't wait. I walked away.

I'd have left the store then and there, but I couldn't go backward through the single-file produce zone, and heading straight for the exit meant I'd have to squeeze past shoppers, cashiers, baggers. I took a deep breath and consulted the list taped to the back of my glove. Once out of the produce section, shoppers were free to fan out. No one was waiting at the meat counter, so I went for it. I ordered the meat, not quite sure why I was bothering, since I didn't have the bok choy, an essential ingredient for my version of beef with oyster sauce. Barb also wanted some feta, and just as I arrived at the dairy section, I heard someone cry out, "That's my cart!" I spun around to see a woman approaching another shopper, who stood next to a cart that was presumably not his.

"I'm so sorry," he said. He was recoiling from both the woman and her cart.

His quick apology did nothing to placate her. She grew belligerent. "That's awful to do," she said. "So irresponsible." She was circling an invisible barrier between her and the man, between her and her cart. She was fearful of him, and of the jar of something with which he had apparently infected her groceries.

Her anger at an honest mistake showed how quickly social graces can disappear when half a face is obscured. Now I understood everyone's hurry. I couldn't get out of that place fast enough. Abandoning my cart next to the empty olive bar, I fled.

When I got home, Barb was sitting at the kitchen table. "Are you okay?" she asked when she saw me. "You were gone for so long. Where are the groceries?"

At once exhausted and keyed up, I wasn't sure I could tell her what had happened without it sounding trivial. "I couldn't get the bok choy," I said. This was true. "So I didn't see the point." This was also true.

"So you didn't buy anything?" She looked confused.

"No," I said. This was true too.

She was quiet. "Ethan, it's okay," she said. "Really, it's fine. We can scrounge up something."

I hoped she wouldn't send me back out there into the world. I hoped she wouldn't ask me to go to the store again. If she did, what would I say?

She didn't ask me to go to the store again, but she did mention more than once that she worried about my state of mind during this period of relative isolation.

"Remind me how old your parents were when they died?" she asked one spring day.

Truth be told, I hadn't given it much thought and had to do a quick calculation, based on the year of the inscription I'd seen in the Dr. Spock book. "Thirty-eight," I said. "At least my mother was thirty-eight. I think they were the same age."

Barb nodded without saying anything. But a few days later, I found a printout on my keyboard. It was a research paper with the title "Anniversary Reactions: Trauma Revisited." And at the top, she'd written, "E: Just something to think about.♥"

The senior author on the paper was her mentor at Temple. As I skimmed the article, phrases like "heightened anxiety" and "lack of control over future negative events" jumped out at me. The whole thing sounded like poppycock—a word, it suddenly occurred to me, that my mother used a lot. By leaving that paper for me to read, Barb appeared to be convinced that as my thirty-eighth birthday on July 20, 2022, drew nearer (which was still more than two years away), and I approached the age my parents were when they died, I would grow increasingly anxious. Then, once the day arrived, full-blown post-traumatic stress would take hold. I didn't buy it. In focusing on this nutty hypothesis of hers, Barb was losing sight of more immediate concerns, such as the boys' health issues.

The boys were picky eaters from day one and weren't gaining any weight. After a great deal of plodding trial and error, I isolated a food allergy. As I sleuthed my way through different food categories, I acted it out like a *Columbo* episode. I'd start to leave the room, then turn and say, very deliberately, hands in pockets, "Just one more thing. . . . I . . . I don't want to appear presumptuous. But there's a distinct possibility that this involves tree nuts." They loved it, as much as kids not given to outward emotion could. I'm pretty sure I saw Sam crack a smile under those hooded eyes of his.

When Barb saw the Columbo act, she wasn't as appreciative as I thought she'd be. "You know, you could save a lot of time if you just took them to an allergist and had patch tests done." She was laughing, which annoyed me. She must have been trying to be helpful by suggesting the allergist, but tests where someone pricks the skin dozens of times, done on children who do not visibly register pain, seemed like an awful idea. Especially during a pandemic.

With all of us at home 24/7, the house was gathering dust more quickly than usual. This was most noticeable in the mornings, when the sun shone through the front windows into the living room, revealing on every dark surface a coating of fine particles a millimeter deep.

Which led me to suspect that dander could be a problem. Mike the Cat was gone, but his dander lingered, embedded in the sofa fabric, the shelves of the linen closet, the bedroom carpets. I went online and ordered a vacuum cleaner with a HEPA filter, as well as new sheets and towels specifically for the boys. I took up the carpet in their room and installed a large air filter. I tried to keep the house as dust-free as possible, but the struggle felt Sisyphean.

"We're going to have to hold off on getting another cat," I said to Barb one afternoon. I gestured to the boys, who were on the couch watching Detective Columbo tell a concert pianist he had a hunch that the musician had murdered his girlfriend and typed up a phony suicide note. It was a sophisticated plot (the forensics involved a manual typewriter); they were engrossed.

She raised her eyebrows. "Are you serious?" she asked.

"We've got the boys," I said. "Isn't that enough?"

Barb shrugged. "Sure, no rush on the cat," she said. "Or we could get one of those bald cats, so Strip doesn't feel like such an oddball."

Now that the landscape I traversed was limited to the rooms in our house, my main concern was the danger lurking therein. I started watching Barb like a hawk when she cooked on the gas burners, double- and triple-checking that she turned them off. If she rolled her eyes, I reminded her that according to Dr. Spock, house fires account for an overwhelming percentage of children's deaths; babies and small children without the wherewithal to escape are at greatest risk.

She was furious when she discovered our firewood was missing from the basement. I had given it all to our next-door neighbor. "Ethan, that's one of the nicest things we do together," she said. "And you're taking *that* away from us? That's just ridiculous."

Looking back on it, I've come to believe that as calm and compassionate as Barb seemed at the time, her tipping point came with the fire ban. I had crossed a line. Her inclination to give me the benefit of the doubt had turned to deep frustration. Even I could sense a Harry Eastlack–like fibrosis taking over, but I didn't know what to do about it.

From behind the closed door of her study, Barb was churning out paper after paper. For years she had made a clear distinction between social isolation and loneliness. It's possible to be socially isolated without feeling lonely. Conversely, you can be in a crowded room and feel insurmountably lonely. I remembered talking with my brother-in-law Rob about his little sister's work at one point, and he quoted a line from the Billy Joel song "Piano Man": "And they're sharing a drink they call loneliness, but it's better than drinking alone." A year earlier, the intersection between loneliness and social isolation was of vague general interest, mostly to people with aging parents and to social services agencies. But now the world was experiencing social isolation on a global scale, not just among locked-in octogenarians but for tens of millions of people, living alone or with people they no longer loved or could no longer communicate with. And, for many, social isolation was quickly shifting into abject loneliness.

Accordingly, Barb's professional reputation was taking off. In fact, she was turning into something of a media star. What had been a topic of passing interest to a handful of academics had become a pressing problem, and journalists turned to Barb, a genial and articulate expert, for insight into the consequences of social isolation as people walled themselves off from the outside world. She was doing a lot of newspaper and radio interviews, often more than one a day, and she kept the door of her study open—pointedly, I believe—as she rattled off a litany of familiar sound bites: ". . . the cumulative effects of social isolation . . ." or ". . . the link between social isolation and depression . . ." or "long-term health consequences."

For my part, I resolutely steered clear of every scrap of news out there, mostly for the boys' sake. Barb became the purveyor of any information that reached me. She tried to give me little daily updates, but after a week or two I suggested we shift to a need-to-know basis. More and more, I was struck by the boys' utter dependence on me. I became their frontline filter. They didn't know how much the world had changed, and I wasn't about to introduce scary phrases like *test positivity rates* into their growing vocabulary.

Maybe Barb equated my lack of interest in the events of the world with a growing lack of interest in her, because after a while she stopped reporting anything at all, even news that was just about her or her work. The boys and I took extra comfort in our bedtime readings of *Anna Karenina*, and I hoped Barb would too. But after a while she opted to stay in the living room to watch the news. I asked her to make sure she switched the channel to PBS—home of the boys' morning TV programs—before going to bed, but she seldom remembered. When I turned on the TV the next day, I clicked out of that madness as quickly as possible.

It shouldn't have come as a surprise, but I was taken aback when I heard Tommy and Sam say something in English for the first time. I considered Tommy the more extroverted of the two and thought he would be first. Instead, it was Sam. We were sitting on the couch watching *Columbo* when I heard Sam say, "Columbo is *ochen umnyy* lieutenant."

Barb was upstairs in her study with the door shut. I nearly went up to deliver this news but thought better of it. On top of the stress of the isolation, our disagreements about best parenting practices were turning our home into a tense terrarium. When she came down about an hour later to fix herself some tea, I told her that Sam had just spoken to me.

"What did he say?" she asked as she passed through the living room on her way to the kitchen. She seemed only mildly interested. She was between interviews.

"He said Columbo is a very intelligent lieutenant. It was a mix of Russian and English."

"Runglish?" she chuckled. She was making a racket in the kitchen, filling the kettle, opening and closing cupboards.

"Runglish. Exactly!"

The next day, it was Tommy who spoke. "Is *ochen* difficult," he replied when I asked him what he thought of English grammar.

"So now you've got a couple of chatterboxes on your hands," Barb said when I reported this additional development to her. "Wow," she added. "What will they be doing next? Inline skating around the living room?"

She didn't have to be churlish about it. "They wouldn't do that," I said.

"Right. I forgot. Too dangerous."

Oddly enough, or perhaps not so surprisingly, the more shut off from the world we became, the more rambunctious the boys got, increasingly more comfortable expressing themselves in their mix of Russian, English, and their own made-up twin language. And they did this in voices that grew louder with each passing month of our confinement. Yet the louder they were, the more she tuned them out.

I'd noticed, too, that Barb's gentle way with the boys had given way to an insensitivity that bordered on gruffness. For instance, she'd come home from her walk, barely say hello, and throw her bag on the couch, paying no attention to whether she risked hitting one of the boys with it. I hoped it was just pandemic-induced frustration. Still, the toss of the bag didn't seem merely careless. There was something almost sinister about it.

She started to head for her study, then stopped. "Ethan, have you stepped outside in the past week?" My silence said everything. I hadn't left the house since the shopping disaster. "I'll read that as a no."

"But what about—" I started to say something about not wanting to leave the boys alone, but she cut me off."

"You can take the boys to the park."

"Which park?"

"The one at the end of the block. There's a playground."

"I'm sure it's still closed," I said. "And what if—"

"What if what?" she asked. She was starting to sound exasperated. "I'm pretty sure the boys have built-in immunities. The research is showing that kids don't get sick very often with this virus, and I think you don't have to worry so much about those two. Right? I mean, they wouldn't play with other kids anyway."

Her head was cocked, as if to signal that whatever I said next would hold the key to my state of mind. I understood what she was saying, of course. But I didn't want to give her the upper hand. So I changed tack. "Even if that playground is open, it has an asphalt surface," I said. "They need to replace it with rubber pavers."

"Ethan, you know that's not an issue, right?"

"Of course it's an issue," I said. "Playground safety is an issue no matter what."

"I know playground safety is an issue in general," she said. "I can't believe we're arguing about this. You're right about the playground surface. Let's write to Philly Parks and Rec and lodge a complaint."

"Now you're talking," I said.

"I'm talking," she said. "But what are you hearing?"

11.

When fall rolled around, Barb reported that parents everywhere were giddy at the prospect of schools reopening. I, on the other hand, had come to believe that homeschooling would be best for Tommy and Sam. I was concerned about what appeared to be the boys' developmental and learning challenges, and I wasn't eager to send them to a school whose teachers were highly unlikely to bother with the translation app, now an indispensable tool in our household. School officials convinced of the importance of assimilation would undoubtedly disapprove of such a tool. Nor was the local elementary school likely to make any of the other necessary adjustments for Tommy and Sam unless a formal alternative education plan was put in place.

I could have tried to mobilize the system of case managers, social workers, and others to help the boys, but the very idea of all that bureaucracy made me cringe. Furthermore, I was pretty sure Tommy and Sam would be targets for bullying; their chances of fitting in with peers were close to nil, and they were just different and vulnerable enough to attract the mean kids. Plus, being from Russia would undoubtedly be a political lightning rod. Bullies have radar for kids like Tommy and Sam. They're geniuses that way.

I told Barb I thought the boys should be homeschooled, at least for a while. By me. She was skeptical and wore an expression I couldn't quite read. Bemusement? Admonishment? Dread?

I quietly stood my ground and continued with the home-schooling, only to find myself vindicated when schools didn't open after all. Barb's university tried reopening, but when a bunch of students got sick, everyone was sent home again. It wasn't until well after the Christmas break that Barb could resume some in-person teaching at Temple. When she did, she seemed overjoyed to be leaving the house.

While I was proud of Barb's professional achievements, I began to feel that the boys and I were competing for her attention and energy. I told myself I was wrong, but I started to detect her pulling away from us in small but unmistakable ways. Television as a family activity stopped, partly because I suggested to Barb that—with her back out in the world—she should keep her distance from the boys. Even after she got her vaccination, Barb said she was too busy for family TV time. If she came home to find me reading *Anna Karenina* to the boys, instead of sitting with us, she went into her study to work. She and I ate dinner late, after the boys had gone to bed, and over our meal I would tell her all about the boys' day. But she just stared at her plate, barely disguising her inattention, tapping on the table with her fingertips, always the same rhythmic taaap tap tap tap, to the precise tempo of the opening of Dvořák's New World Symphony.

I didn't mind being left with the bulk of the child-rearing, really. The boys were becoming my refuge, a source of undivided love and attention, as Barb seemed ever more consumed by work. After all, here I was, being the kind of parent I'd always wished for myself. To my relief, Tommy and Sam didn't gravitate to sports. Aside from my brief fling with baseball while growing up, neither did I. It's almost as if the boys were made to order, syncing up with my own personality as if we actually shared genetic material. We made an interior life for ourselves, one that Barb was only minimally involved in. It was hard to tell whether that was her choice, mine, or the boys', but the shift in family dynamics was unmistakable.

Barb's parents were jubilant when Delmonico's, their favorite restaurant, reopened with a fully redone back patio and invited us out to dinner to celebrate. I didn't feel comfortable entrusting the boys to a babysitter, so I begged off. Barb was incensed.

"This is all just so embarrassing," she said. "You've turned into a total hermit. I'm getting to the point where I'm scared to walk in the door because I never know what you're going to be up to with those two." She was looking in all directions around the room. "The whole house has been turned into a bizarre hypoallergenic classroom. It's just not—"

"I can tidy up," I interrupted. She had a point. The house was stuffed with easels, whiteboards, and other teaching aids, the walls covered with maps and photos of world historical figures: Mao, Lenin, FDR, Churchill.

"It's not about tidying up! Honestly, Ethan, I don't know if you're trying to completely humiliate me or what the hell is going on." Now she was crying, bordering on hysterical. I'd never seen this side of her.

"I'm going to dinner with my parents. Hugs! Laughter! Hearing and seeing in 3D! Seeing people from the neck down, reading body language.

"I don't know what you're going to do. Actually, I have a pretty good idea what you're going to do, but I am going to sit outside at a restaurant and order food. I might even bring home leftovers with traces of nuts and . . . and put them in the refrigerator."

That was definitely out of bounds. I looked over at the boys, who were watching all of this with mounting terror. Even if they couldn't understand all the words, her tone was unmistakable. And kids who grow up in orphanages, I'd read, live in constant fear of conflict, always wary that it could be the harbinger of their removal from their new life and a return to captivity.

I started to say something about the leftovers threat, but she cut me off. "And when my parents ask me why you aren't there, and why you haven't been there on Sunday for God knows how many Sundays, what am I supposed to tell them? The truth? But what is the truth? What *is* the fucking truth, Ethan?"

The curse was jarring—I couldn't remember hearing Barb curse before. And this is the part of the story that begins to be too painful in the retelling, because her anger about my not going to dinner that night marked the start of our undoing. The closer I grew to the boys, the more Barb pulled away and the more contemptuous she became. It was a new side of her. It was as if she knew I would be preoccupied with the boys even before she crossed the threshold, as if I'd left a scent halfway down the block.

• • • •

"Ethan, what the hell is this?" she asked one evening when she walked in the door. The boys and I were seated at the kitchen table doing geography drills. She spotted an EpiPen on the table, picked it up, and was examining it.

"Nothing to worry about," I said, then quickly added, "I mean not yet. I like to keep it within easy reach."

"Okay," she said, drawing both syllables out. "And what are you doing?"

"State capitals." I had a stack of flash cards in front of me, and a large map of the US was tacked to the wall.

"Oh Jesus," she said under her breath but not so much that I wouldn't hear it.

I was not about to apologize to her for what was keeping me so busy. I was beginning to feel like I didn't even know her, the woman I thought I had the luck to fool into marrying me. How could I have so grossly underestimated her capacity for jealousy? I could hardly be faulted for thinking she should get professional help. But there was no reaching her. And here's the irony: she seemed convinced that *I* was the one who couldn't be reached. Talk about role reversals! I was the one who was bringing all the maternal instinct to the marriage, while all Barb seemed to want to do was to climb the academic ladder of tenure and fame.

To my great astonishment, on the very night of the geography drills, Barb demanded that I see a therapist to discuss what she called my "unhealthy attachment" to them. "Barb," I said, trying to keep my tone as measured as possible, although I felt a bubble of rage expanding to fill an air pocket directly behind my sternum. "Shouldn't you be examining your own withdrawal from our family, a family that we decided *together* to build—"

"Okay, forget it," she cut me off. But she couldn't resist adding: "But why do I have the feeling that you're a little like this house?" She gestured with one arm around the walls of the living room in a quick back-and-forth motion like someone on a tear with a paintbrush. "Tug at a corner of wallpaper curling away from the wall, and before you know it, the whole place comes tumbling down." I must have looked at her blankly, because she added, "I can't even begin to keep trying to talk to you about this." And with that she widened the divide that already yawned between us. She shook her head, went into her study, and shut the door.

A few weeks later, we invited Brunch to dinner, our first guest since the boys had come into our lives. Barb went out to pick up Thai food. I had to beg her not to get pad Thai, with all those peanut pieces sprinkled on the top.

Brunch arrived while Barb was still gone.

"Whoa! Ethan!" Brunch said when he saw the boys, who were on the couch watching *Sesame Street*, per Tommy's preference. "This is big. Are you going to introduce us?" Unaccustomed to seeing strangers in the house, the boys looked wary.

"This is Tommy, and this is Sam." I pointed to each of the boys in turn.

Just then, Barb stepped inside, a sturdy plastic bag in each hand.

Brunch was still looking at me and the boys. "Wait. I already forgot. Which one's Tommy and which one's Sam? They look like Xerox copies."

"Tommy is the one with the cap," Barb said. "They could be identical twins, but the only way to know would be DNA testing. And that's—"

"Expensive," Brunch broke in.

"Right," Barb said. "Expensive."

Brunch was grinning. "And maybe it's not even that important," he said. "You'll love 'em, identical or fraternal. Why should it matter? Hey man, people love their kids any way they come."

Brunch didn't stay long after dinner. We walked him to the door. "We've missed you at work, Ethan," he said. He was speaking to me but looking across the room at the boys. He looked preoccupied and uncharacteristically uncomfortable.

After we closed the door, Barb turned to me. She said nothing but held her hands out in front of her, then turned her palms up.

"Ethan, put your hands in my hands." I looked down at her hands, then took them in mine. "Now close your eyes."

I squeezed my eyelids shut. "Are yours closed too?" I asked.

"Maybe. Maybe not," she said. The words were a tease, but the tone was earnest. She was caressing my hands with hers. I was feeling aroused but gathered that was not her intention.

"This is me. Barb," she said. "I'm your wife, and I'm standing here." She guided my right thumb up to her wrist and I felt her strong, rhythmic pulse. "That's my heart, pumping blood in and then out to the rest of my body, which is what creates the warmth you feel in my hands right now. And when you press down on my wrist . . . ." She stopped and waited for me to do just that. "Now you feel the give of my skin, don't you?" I nodded. "And when you open your eyes, what you will see is all of me, breathing in and out. You'll know that I am breathing because you will hear it each time I inhale and each time I exhale, and you will see my chest expanding and contracting. Now open your eyes." I opened them to find her staring into my eyes with an intensity that demanded my attention. But I didn't know what she was expecting of me.

"Was that a séance?" I asked.

"No, it was a reality check," she said.

I suddenly noticed that she looked awful. Her eyes had stopped dancing. Her face had prematurely taken on the angularity of her mother's, but void of the joy. "I know how much they mean to you," she said, and for a moment her eyes softened. Then, as if remembering what she was referring to, they hardened again. Just like that. She flicked her head in the direction of Tommy and Sam, who were too absorbed in Los Lobos singing "Elmo and the Lavender Moon" to register the tension. "But I'm real, and I'm here, and I'm your wife." With that, she turned and went into the kitchen. I heard her fill the teakettle and set it on the burner with a deliberate thwack.

I didn't suspect that she had met someone else. I liked to tell myself that that was out of the question, entirely out of character for Barb. Then again, I no longer trusted my sense of what was *in* character for Barb. And I couldn't entirely rule it out, because I could see the tell of infidelity: the late hours she kept at work, the closed door of her study, the emotional absence.

· · · ·

"Ethan, I think we need to see a therapist," Barb said one day soon after she returned from work. *Aha!* was my immediate thought. *She's finally realized that I'm not the one with the problem.*

But Barb had a different plan in mind. She'd grown increasingly convinced that I was suffering from "the anniversary reaction," and she built her case like a litigator. The anniversary reaction, she said, attempted to explain the "Why now?" of, say, a heart attack on or close to the anniversary of a specific trauma—a psychobiologic response to the recollection of that stressful event. That mentor of hers at Temple who had "discovered" the condition in the 1950s, and coined the term, had made a career-long meal of it. No wonder she was putting such stock in this theory!

In Barb's telling, the phenomenon occurred with such eerie frequency that those who studied it considered it far from coincidental. They believed that the stress of an anniversary could trigger internal mechanisms—probably mediated by changes in levels of cortisol, a major stress hormone—that could eventually lead to tragedy. Barb was convinced that I had triggered my own internal mechanism, and that the closer I got to the age my parents were when they'd died, the greater my peril.

She hadn't mentioned this last summer when she'd left the article for me to read, but she brought it up now as the reason we needed to seek help together, intimating that she was somehow part of the problem. I was thoroughly unconvinced of any of it but agreed to go.

Barb said she would find the marriage counselor, which seemed fair enough, since she was in the psych business. But finding a therapist wasn't as easy as she'd thought. The worldwide crisis had generated a bumper crop of mental illness, and psychologists were in high demand. The crisis had been the perfect trip wire for many couples, who discovered only after being cooped up together for weeks on end that they didn't actually much like each other. And although the surge in telemedicine meant that we could see a therapist in Los Angeles while sitting on our living room couch in Philly, Barb insisted I get out of the house. So it took a while, but eventually she found someone she liked, and she assured me that I'd like him too. His name was Norman Schatz, and he had an office near our house. Going to in-person therapy meant we needed childcare, and since Barb's mother was the only one I trusted to look after Tommy and Sam, Barb asked Bunny to babysit. It was decided: every Wednesday, at 5:30 p.m., we would leave Bunny in charge of the boys and go see Dr. Schatz.

When Bunny arrived before our first session, it was obvious that she was doing her best to act as if everything was perfectly normal. She greeted me tenderly, with a hug that signaled sympathy, perhaps. Or was it pity? I was touched to see that she'd brought a hand-sewn mask not just for herself, but one for each of the boys. She'd made Tommy's from fabric printed with an Elmo motif; Sam's was Big Bird. Yet Bunny's previous lightness was gone. In its place was an expression of studious neutrality. She'd brought her own dinner—a sandwich wrapped in wax paper—and a plaid thermos filled with tea, which she set on the kitchen table before she settled onto the couch with the boys to watch TV.

Before that first appointment, I had been a bit skeptical. Had Barb chosen someone she knew to be sympathetic to her point of view? Or maybe, as a member of the same Fraternity of Psych, had she spoken to Dr. Schatz before our meeting in order to work the ref? But as soon as I met Dr. Schatz, my concerns melted away. I liked him immediately. He was in his late sixties with a slight paunch, a full head of wavy gray hair, and wire-rimmed glasses that made me miss my own—and resent Barb a little for having foisted those trendy tortoiseshell frames on me. Dr. Schatz wore a brown tweed jacket and khakis with a couple of prominent grease stains. His brown leather belt was creased in a way that made it clear he tightened and loosened it with the tides of his girth. He wore a thick gold wedding band. He was calm and kind, with a placid smile that would disarm the wariest of clients. A Jewish Fred Rogers.

I thought Dr. Schatz's office would be bright and airy, with sunlight pouring through the windows, exuding a spirit intended to cheer even the darkest of souls. Instead, it was like a womb. The hardwood floor was covered by one of the largest area rugs I'd ever seen (after a certain point, why not just install wall-to-wall?), a kilim in hues of rusted red and marine blue. Even the floor and table lamps scattered around the room didn't do much to lighten things up. It was well into spring, and still light outside, but the room was dark. Under one window was a hulking wooden desk with lots of drawers, piled high with papers, file folders, and books. Even the antique desk chair had a pile on it. It was clear that Dr. Schatz spent most of his time in his leather recliner, a well-worn Stressless from Scandinavia. Barb and I had considered buying one while shopping for living room furniture, then rejected it as too modern. Now I envied Dr. Schatz's level of comfort. Every time he sank down into that chair, I imagined him fighting the urge to nap. This contrasted with the picture Barb and I must have presented, parked awkwardly opposite him on the edge of a large dark-brown couch. It was probably upholstered in something soft like chenille, but to me it felt like a scratchy wool sweater that becomes intolerable a few seconds after putting it on. We wore masks when we walked in but removed them after reconfirming that everybody was vaccinated.

Maybe I was wrong about the room. Maybe it had started out bright and sunny but with the years had absorbed the darkness of its patients, leaving them lighter, leavened. There was the law of conservation of energy, so why shouldn't there be a law of conservation of light? Such a theory was something I might once have mused about to Barb during my period of nonstop chatter after we first got together, when I told her pretty much anything that came to mind. Then she would have been amused and would have asked me to expound. But now our interactions were minimal and robotic, restricted to logistics, shopping lists, and home repairs.

Dr. Schatz started out by asking how our time both in and now out of isolation was going. Barb wanted to dive straight back into the fray of humanity, return to classroom teaching, go to conferences, ride on buses, while I was "glued in place," as she put it.

He turned to me. "Ethan, is that how you'd describe it?"

"I guess," I said. "I'm not really feeling the urge to go out. And we have two sons that need a lot of attention—"

"Oh my God," said Barb.

"They're twins," I told Dr. Schatz.

"Could we please table the boys for now?" Barb asked.

"Sure," I said.

Barb started in on her speech, and Dr. Schatz did nothing to stop her. It was clear that she'd spent considerable time rehearsing her opening testimony; I wondered if she'd watched herself in a mirror to polish her delivery. She began by summing up the facts, from my parents' death onward. It was oddly fascinating to hear myself being referred to in the third person. I was impressed by how much she knew, considering how little we'd actually discussed it. Next, she laid out her anniversary-reaction diagnosis. She asked Dr. Schatz if he was familiar with the phenomenon. "Yes," he replied. "I'm quite familiar with it."

Since there was no need to define it for Dr. Schatz, she turned to me. A main feature of the anniversary reaction, she explained, was that people who suffer from it keep both the problem and the efforts to deal with it to themselves. This was certainly a convenient explanation for Barb, as it covered all my issues in one handy diagnosis.

The trigger, Barb said, is a time associated with a prior traumatic event, consciously or unconsciously selected by the patient.

The painful impact of the event might fade from consciousness, but the destructive forces lie in wait until the triggering event sets them in motion. In my case, it would be when I turned thirty-eight.

As Barb saw it, my thirty-eighth birthday was headed straight for me, like a heat-seeking missile. And as that happened, she could see me drifting into what she had the temerity to term an unhinged state. Moreover, she said, when it came to my attachment to the boys, it was not coincidental that they were the age I was when my parents died.

All of this struck me as over-the-top, especially given the fact that I hadn't given Barb the slightest reason to believe that the anniversary of my parents' death had anything to do with my state of mind. If I had been struggling psychologically, I'd have argued that the reasons had everything to do with Barb shutting the emotional doors that had once so magically connected us. And she did the same with the boys. I found my attention drifting, my mind's eye returning to the house, to the living room, to Bunny and how she and the boys might be getting on. Were they dazzling her with their ever-improving English? Trying to teach her a little Russian?

Before our first meeting, I'd assumed that as a man, Dr. Schatz might be more likely to side with me, that I would be able to convince him that Barb was a caricature of a career woman, uninterested in her family. I was further convinced that the kindly Dr. Schatz would point out to Barb that entering into couples' therapy having pre-diagnosed one of the parties might not be the most effective way to "find a path forward," as a therapist might put it. But maybe she'd set the whole thing up, including (maybe) going to the trouble of finding a therapist who was familiar with the anniversary thing, making him complicit in this cockamamie idea.

But he sided with neither of us. Couples therapists, I now understand, are excellent diplomats, in a constant dreary struggle to refrain from taking sides. "Have you mentioned this hypothesis to Ethan before today?" he asked Barb with studied disinterest.

"Yes," she said. "But I thought we should continue the conversation in a safe place. A place that felt safe to Ethan. And to me."

Then he looked straight at me: "Ethan, is this something you're concerned about?"

"No."

Barb interjected. "But we've talked about it."

Yes, I knew when my parents had died. And yes, I knew I was going to turn thirty-eight someday. But I had no recollection of having mentioned a connection of any kind to Barb. As far as I was concerned, Barb was hoisting herself on a petard of psychobabble.

I felt myself getting angry. Barb was the one who was distancing herself during what she claimed was a critical time in my life. If I were truly in danger of some kind of spontaneous psychiatric combustion, wouldn't she want to be closer to me? Here she was, with a PhD in psychology, building a case on the flimsiest of evidence. I was beginning to feel like the pro here, not Barb.

Dr. Schatz offered an assessment.

"It seems that the two of you have landed in opposite camps," he said. "Barb, from what I'm hearing, you're a people person. And getting back to normal life sounds like something you'd like to do as soon as possible." Barb was nodding. She was also starting to sniffle; she lifted her right hand to her face and swiped quickly beneath both eyes. Seeing her like that put a lump in my throat. I had to look away.

Dr. Schatz continued. "What we're finding is that after the world begins opening back up, people are placing exaggerated importance on what they valued before. Also, and this might be more relevant here, people's personalities and proclivities often emerge from crises in more pronounced form."

My tendency appeared to be toward reclusiveness. No argument there. And I was grateful to him for avoiding the word *agoraphobic*, a word that Barb had fired in my direction more than once. Now, more than ever, my "anticipatory anxiety," as he put it, was directed at going outside. Barb was nodding again, this time minus the tears.

I was listening to this through a scrim of vague panic. I had dismissed Barb's anniversary-reaction postulation, but Dr. Schatz's theory sounded entirely plausible. It also sounded like he was describing something that was unfixable. Adrenaline surged through the backs of my hands. My interior monologue, which had over the months been building into a quiet terror, was now being given voice by this avuncular man who sat just a few feet across from me. Now my mind was stilled. I heard nothing but the sound of a small electric clock purring on a side table next to me.

Barb no doubt thought that in the safe space of Dr. Schatz's office, I would open up, that we would have breakthroughs. But over the ensuing weeks, things only got worse. Every time we crossed the threshold of Dr. Schatz's darkened chamber, I felt my heart close in on itself. During sessions, Barb and I started speaking not to each other but only to Dr. Schatz, which even

I—therapy novice that I was—understood to be a step in the wrong direction. We were inching away from each other on the couch, a retreat that surely didn't escape Dr. Schatz's notice. I fantasized about markers on that sofa measuring our growing separation—perhaps when the distance hit ten yards, he'd declare a first down and let us end this torture.

At the start of our fourth, and last, session, Barb announced, "We need to talk about the elephant in the room." I looked at Dr. Schatz, who looked first at me, then at Barb. "Tommy and Sam," she said.

Now I was enraged. I addressed Barb directly, for the first time since we had begun seeing Dr. Schatz. "Barb, did you ever really want kids? Or was your career all that mattered after all? I thought you'd be a better mother."

I had ignited a fuse. She turned to me, her face flaming hot. "You're so wrong, Ethan. My desire to parent is completely irrelevant. You were the one who was conflicted about having kids. I'd be happy to be the mother of . . . of . . . ." Now she was stammering. "The whole thing just exploded. You've built this whole world around these two . . . two . . . . You've lost your grip . . . you're . . . ." She was crying, unable to finish her thought. She leaned over, picked up her bag from the floor, rose from the couch, and walked out the door.

• • • •

Nearly four years after we said those "I wills" in front of a hundredsome people and all those freakish body parts at the Mütter Museum, I walked into the kitchen for coffee one morning to find Barb standing next to the refrigerator. The door of the fridge was open. I had the presence of mind not to ask her to close it.

"Ethan, I'm done," she said. She was the color of bone. "I should never have done this." What she meant by "this" was unclear. Her voice was low, in a minor key I associated with terrible sadness. "What misguided impulse made me bring home those two . . . ," and she stopped. Then she started again: "I don't know where you've gone," she said. "I don't know where to find you." Her voice lingered in the air, like an afterimage. The silence grew into white noise. I welcomed it and prayed Barb wouldn't speak again, because if she didn't speak there would be silence, and in silence there can be hope. I felt hot, and my heart was beating so fast it seemed ready to send shards of itself in every direction. I was standing erect but felt an inward slumping, like a volcano's summit, the rim and walls detaching and dropping downward into the crater.

But instead of hopeful, the silence that hung between us was ominous, hard at the edges. I wanted to say everything, but, going against my every impulse, I said nothing. In hindsight, what did it matter? I had made my greatest mistake years earlier, and for years thereafter, in my belief that laying bare my truths would give her second thoughts. What I didn't understand then, but perhaps do now, is that in my silence lay the seeds of self-destruction. Even then, I couldn't stop myself from robbing the present to repay the debts of the past.

I insisted that we both sit down together with the boys to explain what was happening. All Barb could do was stare at them, tears streaming down her cheeks, so I did the talking. I used the translation app, just to make sure they understood every single word of what I needed to convey. Even with the help from the app, both boys looked confused. Sam, on his regular spot on the couch, kept his eyes cast downward. Tommy maintained his steady gaze and asked only one question, which happened to be exactly what I was wondering: When would she be back? Barb sighed, a long guttural expelling of breath. I worried for a fraction of a second that she might do something to harm them, so much did she seem to resent them now. Instead, she maintained a studied distance, acting as if she barely knew them.

Barb went to live with some friends from graduate school, taking all her personal things with her, objects that didn't mean much while she was there but that left a big blank space after they were gone: her electric toothbrush that always sat, collecting grime, in its charger; her favorite canvas tote bags, one from the 2012 American Psychological Association meeting, where she first presented her loneliness findings, another from the Barnes Collection, covered with Van Gogh's misshapen houses. And the shoes: running shoes, rain boots, flats, and pumps I'd spent years stepping over—all gone. I kept finding strands of long reddish hair attached to everything. I tried not to look for them, but there they were, threaded across the shower drain or stuck on the back of the sofa. She did leave a few possessions that predated us. I couldn't tell whether she did that by way of consolation or because this was a separation and not a divorce. In my darker moments I had the dreadful notion that she intended those objects to loom large, a big angry exclamation point. One particularly painful reminder was the one-eyed stuffed duck. At first I thought she'd taken it, because it was no longer in its usual position on the bed; then I spotted it under the bed. It had dust bunnies clinging to it. I plucked off the skeins of dust and set the duck back in its usual place, nestled between two pillows. But seeing it there made my chest feel so heavy I was having trouble breathing. I took the duck into the living room and put it on a bookshelf. Still, wherever I was in the room, I felt that black button eye staring at me accusingly. I moved it to a higher shelf and turned it around, facing the other way. After that, whenever I walked into the living room, I tried to avoid looking in the direction of the bookshelf.

12.

AFTER BARB LEFT, ROUTINES MATTERED MORE THAN EVER. I came to rely on them to get through my day: preparing the boys' lessons, giving them their lessons; preparing their meals, giving them their meals.

I was still in disbelief that Barb had forced this impossible choice on me: my wife or my children. Confused, I felt an all-consuming remorse. But what did I have to be remorseful about? Surely Barb was of the opinion that I had driven her out. But just as surely she had to know, in her heart of hearts, that I was doing my best to be there for two children whose many special needs had to come before ours.

An adherence to strict regimen became my salvation. I made the bed the instant I got up, neatly but with a corner folded open so that I could slide right back in at night. I still slept on my side of the bed but piled Barb's side with laundry and magazines. I put dirty dishes in the sink throughout the day and filled it one-third

of the way with water and a teaspoon of dish detergent. I waited
to wash the dishes until the boys went to bed. I dusted the house
from top to bottom once a day and vacuumed before breakfast and
after dinner. Though marooned in the house—with groceries and
other essentials delivered—I told myself that the boys and I were
better off.

But after several months of this, I noticed an odd, suffocating
claustrophobia creeping up on me, as if the house were involut-
ing, the walls inching closer to wherever I happened to be. I
needed to get out. Really out. Out of the house. Out of Philly.
Out of Pennsylvania. I thought about an extended road trip with
the boys, but Barb now had the car, and besides, I suspected that
Tommy might be prone to car sickness. I rejected a dozen more
possibilities, until suddenly one morning I had an idea. I'd take
the boys on a Hill and Dale bike trip! After that first trip, Hill
and Dale glossy catalogs began showing up with the mail on a
regular basis. During the global furlough, they'd stopped coming. I assumed the company hadn't made it, but when I looked
them up online, I discovered that they were still in business, and
Italy rides were being offered again for the first time that summer. In addition to the usual marketing hype ("sun-drenched
hills"), there was an equal dose of clinical reassurance ("frequent
testing," "vaccination required," "guest pods"). If the goal was
to simultaneously entice and calm, they hit the sweet spot. I was
sold, and I began to find myself even getting a bit excited.

I decided not only to return to Italy, but back to Piedmont, the
same region Barb and I had cycled through on our honeymoon.
After all, it was a tried-and-true route. Why risk more of the
unknown than was absolutely necessary? The stops along the way

were beautiful, the food delicious. Of course, Tommy and Sam wouldn't be able to enjoy the food part; I'd have to pack their meals. But that seemed a minor burden. Barb and Dr. Schatz would undoubtedly have their own explanations for my decision to return to Italy, speculating about "repetition compulsion" and other notions dreamed up by Freud and Friends.

When I suggested the idea to the boys, they seemed completely gung ho. They listened politely as I explained my reasons for choosing a trip I'd already taken. I was so eager to tell them everything about the first trip that every night, instead of reading to them (after finishing *Anna Karenina*, for a healthy dose of American history we had moved on to *Gone with the Wind*), I told them bedtime stories about the previous adventure. I described the church bells, the monastery turned luxury hotel (I omitted the story of the sabotaged bikes), the bustling Italian villages, the stunning views from the crest of every hill. I devoted an entire bedtime to the story of Sarah and Luigi, the guides who were stealthily a pair. I described how Barb's sixth sense about people and her Columbo-like skills had led to her decoding of that romance. The boys didn't roll their eyes the way I'm told kids usually do when their parents start reminiscing. I swear, when I told them those stories, they came alive.

"Will it be just like that when we go?" Tommy asked.

"I hope so," I said. I had no clue what the answer to this was, but I happened to be wondering the very same thing myself.

The boys were accustomed to having me as their mainstay, so it wouldn't be strange that we'd be taking this trip without Barb. It was hard for me to know how they processed the fact that she was no longer a presence in their lives, and I was reluctant to dig deeply. Sometimes, I thought, the unexamined life might be best—particularly with kids as fragile as Tommy and Sam.

The staff at Hill and Dale's Austin headquarters were as accommodating this time around as the first. Having helped build a customer-facing business myself, I appreciated all that went into this level of service.

My reservation coordinator was Debra, who informed me that I was still in the computer system. This meant that she knew my jersey size, as well as the dimensions of the bike frame I'd need. Since neither boy had learned to ride a bike, I planned to attach a small trailer to my bike and pull them along. When I told Debra I'd be bringing my own bike trailer for towing my two sons, she was impressed but pointed out that, given the extra weight and the hilly terrain, an e-bike might be a good idea. "There's no charge to upgrade to an e-bike," she said cheerfully. Since my last trip, she said, e-bike technology had come a long way. "You'll soar up those hills," she added. Soaring up a hill sounded like something the boys might enjoy. Besides, since that first trip with Barb, the elegant engineering that went into bike design now interested me and I was eager to learn the mechanism behind it. As I pondered the notion of an e-bike, Debra said, "And Barb's bike? Same as last time?"

Okay, that was a database bug in need of fixing. They couldn't simply assume that the same two people who traveled together four years earlier would be traveling together now. I started compiling a mental list of issues to raise with the company. "She won't be coming on this one," I said matter-of-factly. "She's been having health problems." It sounded wrong as soon as I said it.

"Oh, I'm so sorry to hear that," Debra said. I cringed.

I quickly changed the subject. "My sons have dietary restrictions," I said.

"Oh, that shouldn't be a problem. And their jersey sizes? A child's small? And we can have mediums on hand in Italy if they need to swap them out."

"Yeah, that should be fine," I said, still distracted by her Barb faux pas.

To prevent any more uncomfortable phone conversations with the well-meaning people at Hill and Dale, I started sending emails to the company's "guest experience" team. I listed the boys' particular problems: Tommy's and Sam's food allergies and both boys' delicate constitutions—which mandated that they stay out of the rain no matter what. I needed Hill and Dale's assurance that at mealtime, the boys would be seated directly next to me. How they spaced the other guests was their business. I tried to keep the emails to a minimum so as not to be a bother, but I also knew that failing to inform them of each and every issue could be disastrous. I printed out the emails and put them in a file folder to take with me. *You can never be too safe*, I thought. If someone had pointed out to me that I might have been on a quixotic quest to recreate the magical time Barb and I had on our honeymoon, I'd have scoffed at that. My rationale (or so I told myself) for choosing an identical trip was not just to show the boys the beauty of the Italian countryside but to reveal to them that the world out there was characterized by good and light, too, not just the bleakness of a Russian orphanage—or, for that matter, the pandemic-era home of a fractured marriage.

Barb came by one day to pick up a few more things (the duck, which she must have seen on the shelf in the living room, remained behind) and to "see how I was doing." "Fine," I told her.

"We're just fine." I made a point of emphasizing the "we" part. I didn't tell her about the trip.

I ordered the boys' trailer. When it arrived in Philly, I could see it was intended for children far younger than Tommy and Sam, so it was a good thing the boys were light for their age. I hitched it to my own bike, and the boys and I took it for a trial spin around the block. It was perfect. I also bought an oversized carrier that attached nicely to my back.

A few weeks before our departure, trip-related paraphernalia started showing up in the mail. Hill and Dale sent waivers to sign and a glossy day-by-day itinerary to read. It looked like the company was using nearly the exact route through Piedmont that Barb and I had taken four years earlier.

I knew the food on the trip couldn't be trusted, even if I ordered special meals for the boys, so I prepared eight days' worth of meals for each of them, avoiding anything perishable. I packed their trailer in a box and checked it at the airport.

The flight to London was packed. With the latest surge behind us, the whole world had started traveling again, everyone feeding a pent-up desire to be going somewhere. Yet even with the lull in the pandemic, the procession of troubling variants had created an atmosphere of chronic vigilance. Accordingly, our seats on the plane were in the new Janus configuration I'd been hearing about, with the middle seat backward and all of the seats wrapped in a shell of transparent plexiglass. We landed at Heathrow at daybreak, three hours before the flight to Turin.

Most people inside the terminal were masked. A few wore plastic shields, which we'd seen on the flight too. I was looking forward to showing Tommy and Sam the same Fortnum & Mason bar that Barb had introduced me to years earlier. I was sure I knew just where it was: Terminal 5, Level 2, Gate A18. I took us straight there. But it was gone. Exhausted and grumpy, both boys tugged at me, pleading with me to go straight to the gate. The missing café made me wonder if I had imagined the whole thing—the teal-blue stools, the menu with all that caviar, the bone china saucer and cup the coffee was served in.

On the flight to Turin, even when I craned my neck every which way from my window seat, I saw no mountains, no ribbons of river, just bland countryside, more browns than blues and greens. Had the pandemic wiped out mountains and rivers too?

It was midafternoon by the time we arrived at the hotel. The check-in went smoothly. I didn't want to do anything too pathetic, like request the same room Barb and I had stayed in, though I remembered that it was Room 428. The boys and I were given a different room. Almost immediately upon opening the door, I missed Barb with a homesick yearning that felt like a kick to the gut.

For dinner, I unpacked a meal for the boys and ordered room service for myself. My meal was left outside the room. We all slept deeply. The boys would have slept until noon, but I got them up early to pack and get ready. I made certain they both wore their Gore-Tex jackets, but I still checked the local weather report frequently. It called for sun all day. So far so good.

We went downstairs to the lobby early and I found three chairs for us in a far corner next to a sunny window. I worried fleetingly that we might see people from the last trip—or, more likely, the same guides—who were bound to wonder where Barb was. But I tried to push that worry from my mind. I did see one guide, wearing the same signature Hill and Dale jersey as mine. I didn't recognize him. We made eye contact briefly, but he hurried out the front door, looking like he'd forgotten something.

I looked out the window just as two long-limbed sleek young women dressed like fashion models (although it was barely 9:00 a.m.) passed by. One of them turned toward me. She stopped and said something to her companion, who also peered in, looking first at me, then at Tommy and Sam, who sat in chairs across from me. As they walked on, I could swear I saw one of them shaking her head. A ripple of something akin to fear hit my stomach.

I remembered that I needed to reconfigure the translation app to go straight from Italian to Russian and started rummaging in my backpack for my phone. Tommy and Sam were watching me lazily. I had hoped they'd catch my excitement on this first morning of a Hill and Dale bike trip, but they just looked bored, as if they'd already seen everything they needed to see. I found the phone in the backpack but kept my head down, hoping that when I looked up again I would no longer be overwhelmed by an unshakable feeling that this trip, which I'd planned so painstakingly and with such anticipation, was a terrible mistake.

Part Two

Italy

July 17, 2022

Dear Pearl,

I'm back in Turin, and tomorrow morning we head out to the hills around Piemonte. Even though it's a different part of Italy from your Italy, I'm still excited about cycling through villages that might look like Sersale. And I promise that for every *baci di dama* I eat, I'll pretend it's one of your delicious *ginetti*.

It's my first time on this route, but the three other guides I'm with have done it a few times. It's two guys and another girl. Her name is Chiara, and she's from Calabria! I asked her if she knew Sersale, and she said no (she's a city girl).

And I have news! I've made a summer resolution to stop sulking about losing you and stop feeling so shattered that I didn't get to say goodbye and to just be grateful that I had you for as long as I did. I do count my blessings for that. So many of my friends never even had the chance to get to know their grandparents.

Even though I won't be able to mail this letter from "our" post office on President Street, I can post it from anywhere, really, because you're everywhere. I'll find the perfect spot. And I know it will make its way to you, just like all the others do.

Mi manchi tanto.

Love,

Izzy

13.

It was barely 9:00 a.m. and the cool air in the van was already succumbing to the shadeless heat outside. Izzy climbed in and settled herself in the back. She opened a bag of trail mix and started picking out fat golden sultanas, popping them into her mouth one by one. Chiara had her head bent over her phone, her thumbs dancing in Italian. Ben was checking the Garmins before putting them on the bikes to make sure they were all showing the correct GPS coordinates for Day One. They were waiting for Travis. The last Izzy had seen him, he'd looked like he was headed for the hotel lobby.

"Shit, it's hot in here," Ben said, and he gave the door handle a firm thump with the butt of his palm. As soon as the door slid open, there stood Travis. He fairly catapulted himself inside, trailed by a frenetic energy. For Travis to display anything beyond total calm was rare. He was so unflappable that Ben had once suggested that Travis had emerged from his mother's womb in a T-shirt printed with the words "Born to Chill." So to see Travis that morning looking like he'd just encountered a ghost or a grizzly made the others snap to attention. Chiara and Ben looked up. Izzy stopped mid-chew.

"We have an AGC and you're not going to believe this one," Travis said, slightly out of breath, which was also strange for someone in such sinewy good shape. Had he sprinted the few hundred feet from the hotel out to the van?

AGC was the code that the Hill and Dale guides used to remind themselves that living creatures are All God's Children, even those Hill and Dale guests who insisted on changing hotel rooms (out of a fixed belief that hotels always try to get away with giving you a lesser room first, and unless you call them on it you'll wind up in rooms next to elevator banks and air shafts), whose water in their water bottles wasn't cold enough, who disliked the vegetarian selection at lunch or the slow service at dinner, who complained that the roads were too busy or had too many potholes, who found their bikes too heavy when compared to their monocoque carbon fiber frames at home. These were the people the guides wanted to send back to the States on the next plane out of Milan or Stockholm or Hanoi. But the company's corporate mantra, buttressed by regular reminders from Austin headquarters, made clear that all Hill and Dale guests—even the most annoying, entitled, high-maintenance among them—had their own unique needs, which, if humanly possible, should be met. Pretty soon, among the guides, All God's Children transmogrified into All God's Credit Cards, as in "All God's Credit Cards are honored here at Hill and Dale."

Every trip had at least one AGC. Sometimes they came in pairs, married couples who didn't merely reinforce each other's complaints but amplified them. People with post-pandemic stress were, of course, a new class of squeaky wheel. They were the ones who decided a hotel wasn't taking sufficient safety measures, that it wasn't enough to have personalized water bottles and hand sanitizers for every guest, that a restaurant's tables weren't spaced far enough apart, that another guest had coughed. Or at the opposite end of the dissatisfaction spectrum were those who complained that Hill and Dale was *too* restrictive when it came to contagion precautions. "I didn't come all this way to have to stay a mile away from everyone," said one unhappy guest on a newly restarted trip through Normandy. Still, no matter the complaint, all judgment about guests stayed in the hermetically sealed confines of the staff circle—or, on that morning, the sacred, stifling space that was the inside of the Hill and Dale guides' Sprinter van.

At nine o'clock on the first morning of every weeklong ride, guests assembled in the lobby of the hotel in their bike shorts and the red-and-white Hill and Dale jerseys sent to them in advance of the trip, though many of them preferred to show up in alternative jerseys, advertising a 200-mile ride they had just cycled in Eugene, Oregon, or a triathlon recently completed in Denver. Prior to that first morning, any special requirements had been handled in Austin by guest-services staff, who'd forwarded the requests to the guides on the ground. Then it was up to the guides to fulfill the requests, however ridiculous they might seem. The company was working hard to rebuild the business, which meant that the word *no* did not exist at Hill and Dale. Or, if uttered, it was to be followed quickly by *problem*. A hypoallergenic pillow at every stop? No problem. A lumbar cushion at every meal, or SIM card–loaded cell phone upon arrival? No problem.

Travis cleared his throat. "I don't know whether to laugh or just flip out on this guy and call Austin," he said, then added, "or find the closest psych ward."

Chiara looked confused. Ben, who was from Long Island but had spent a semester in Rome, leaned toward her and translated: "*Ospedale psichiatrico*." Chiara's expression changed to alarm. "Really?" she asked, her sweet voice a delicate bell filling the van.

"It's the guy from Philadelphia," Travis said, shaking his head. He opened his mouth to speak but no words came out, and in less than a second he was laughing so hard that, whenever he tried to compose himself enough to speak, his words were engulfed by another gale of laughter. Then, to Izzy's bewilderment, a mirth contagion hit and Ben was also laughing, with Chiara following his lead. Izzy waited for Travis to say more, but he didn't.

"The one with his sons? Are they no-shows?" Izzy intended the question partly to fill the verbal void and partly to interrupt the circuit of laughter. No-shows were rare—the trips were prepaid and the refund window always ended a week before they began. Besides, Travis wouldn't be hyperventilating about a guest who didn't show. Which made his answer all the more surprising. "I . . . I guess you could say that," Travis said, wiping his eyes with the back of his hand.

The main office had alerted the guides that the guy from Pennsylvania, a returning guest named Ethan Fawcett who'd reserved spots for himself and his two young sons, might be trouble. One of his boys had nut allergies so severe that all products containing nut traces had to be expunged. Even nut dust in the air could be a problem. But the nut issue was just the beginning. Both boys ate only a few specific foods, which none of the hotels in Piedmont, Italy, a region known for its sophisticated cuisine, were likely to have on hand. So Mr. Fawcett had informed the staff that he would bring his children's meals for the week, which had to stay refrigerated. And there was more: If it rained, which was improbable but not unprecedented for that region of Italy at that time of year, under no circumstances could the boys get wet. Their father was bringing sturdy rain gear, but he was emphatic about protecting his children from precipitation.

After a minute or so, Travis was finally calming down. He was scanning the inside of the van as if it were his first time in it, not the second home it had become for the four of them that summer. Izzy followed his gaze as it took in the seats streaked black with bike lube and the floor littered with Snickers and Kinder Bueno wrappers.

"Those kids are unreal . . ." he managed to spit out, his larynx choked by mirth.

"What do you mean?" Ben asked.

"Not here . . ." Travis sat on the edge of a plastic tub filled with bike parts, holding his head in his hands.

Chiara looked mystified. Ben was scowling and asked, "You mean we went to all that trouble sending every walnut to fucking Timbuktu and he came alone? Oh, man."

"I didn't say he came alone," Travis said. He broke off again. Then he looked straight at Izzy, his safest harbor. Izzy tried to read his meaning from his eyes, but the message was too garbled.

"What are you even saying?" Ben asked.

But Travis was already out of the van with his clipboard, and the rest were scampering after him toward the hotel. In the lobby there was no mistaking the Hill and Dale guests: they couldn't have looked more out of place in the lobby of a luxury hotel than if they had been a gathering of circus clowns. They all wore skin-tight black Lycra shorts, and most were clomping around in bicycle cleats. "Toddlers with a load," a guide had once said of the cushioned derrieres. Already that summer, Izzy had heard dozens of acidic comments from her coworkers. Their joking made her uncomfortable. They were employed to help people, not make fun of them. Whenever the jokes started, Izzy stayed quiet.

She spotted Ethan Fawcett immediately, in a corner, the darkest part of the room, seated in a wingback chair, his head down as he fussed with his backpack. He was a slight, handsome man, with a thick head of wavy brown hair. Already isolated from the group, Izzy thought, and the week had barely begun. In keeping with their special status, AGCs were frequently "assigned" to a specific guide, either back in Austin (if the clues were strong enough) or in the first hours of a trip. As lead guide, Travis took on the loudest complainers, the most likely to disturb the group's equilibrium. Ben, a bike-tech genius, got the "fixers," people constantly asking to have their tires filled or adjustments made to their brake sensitivity, rear derailleur, or seat height. Chiara got the food and culture snobs. And Izzy took the fragile and sensitive ones. If someone fell far behind the pack, it was Izzy who would circle back to stay with them. Or if guests were traveling solo and had trouble connecting with the group, it was Izzy who rode with them and sat next to them at dinner.

When Izzy saw the guest from Philadelphia sitting by himself like that, she knew that unless she crossed the lobby and welcomed him, no one would. Facing him, and sunk into two shorter wing chairs, were his sons, knitted caps on the backs of their heads visible just above the chairs. They sat perfectly still. No squirming. Unusually well-behaved. That part felt like a blessing.

From across the room Izzy couldn't make out what was odd, what had made Travis double over with laughter.

She felt a familiar anticipation, not unlike the feeling she used to get as a girl when she was reading a book and could tell that an illustration was coming on the next page, a realization she absorbed with pleasure and dread. She desperately wanted the image she was conjuring to be the same as the illustrator's. If the paper was thin enough, she would hold the page to the light, then slowly turn it and study the drawing for a good long time. Sometimes the drawings were so wrong that Izzy wondered if the illustrator had even read the book.

Now, as she approached the little family in the corner of the room, she noticed something about the parallax view of the boys' heads that was throwing her depth perception off. With each step closer, the boys weren't blossoming in three dimensions as her eye expected them to. Her brain, so entrenched in the normal, started sending alarms while struggling to make sense of the increasingly discordant scene. *Oh no*, she thought. *They're both disabled.* This was going to be a bad week. Why hadn't Travis told them? And why was that riotously funny? And, for heaven's sake, why hadn't anyone in Austin caught this before allowing two disabled children on the trip, two children and a dad who, by now, she was coming to understand, would be her charge for the week?

Reflexively, she looked to her left to more fully take in the two angelically behaved impaired children, still not stirring. She was a hunter making her way through the woods, silently approaching her prey when, with no warning at all, a branch snapped overhead, the crack so loud it nearly knocked her legs out from under her. Unconsciously, she lifted her hand to her clavicle to touch her grandmother's cross.

She thought her brain was just having trouble squaring itself with her eyes. But in the next second—was it a full second?—she understood what Travis meant. They were, in fact, unreal. Literally. They were cut-out figures, two large sturdy pieces of cardboard, fully dressed in bright-green matching Gore-Tex parkas and rain pants.

Ambient sounds suddenly struck Izzy as at once too loud and disquietingly garbled. She struggled to breathe and felt like she was moving through water. She tried to offer no sign to onlookers that something was terribly wrong. She could feel Travis tracking her movements—and not just Travis. A lot of people were watching her as she approached the man and his life-size paper-doll boys, marooned in the corner of the lobby of the Palazzo Righini Hotel in Turin, Italy. She became aware of a shift taking place in the room, as more of the Hill and Dalers came to appreciate the scene, obviously gawking while pretending not to.

Once the state of things grew clear and nonnegotiable, Izzy found herself oddly in tune with the little scene. She avoided looking at the two chairs and walked straight up to Ethan Fawcett, wearing her best Hill and Dale greeter smile.

"Are you Ethan?" He had earbuds in and was focused intently on rummaging through his backpack. He didn't notice her, even when she stood just a few inches away.

She leaned down and tapped him gently on the shoulder. He looked up, his full brown eyes meeting hers almost languidly. As soon as he did, she felt a softening. He didn't seem visibly startled or in the least disturbed, and he offered something close to a smile, combined with a solicitous nod, as if to ask what he might do for her, since she was so clearly planted there, requesting his attention.

"I'm Izzy, one of the guides."

"Nice to meet you, Izzy," Ethan said. She took a step back as he stood up to shake her hand. "This is Tommy." He pointed to one of the two figures in the chairs opposite him. Then Ethan nodded at the other chair. The corners of Ethan's eyes were crimped, his forehead a plane marked by premature creases. "And that's Sam. Forgive them if they don't say hello. We're all pretty jet-lagged." His manner was kindly yet guarded.

Now she could see the boys straight on. Their faces were black-and-white photographic portraits. Sam had a serious, old-soul look. Although he was clearly just a boy, his face reminded her of a daguerreotype she'd once seen of a handsome young Civil War soldier. Tommy was smiling, bemused, mischievous, clearly a charmer. He'd be a lady-killer someday, she found herself thinking. Then she caught herself. They weren't real. From the way they were seated, they appeared to be hinged at the hips and knees and she wondered if Ethan had created them himself. In the space of seconds, her professional obligation and personal empathy jostled for position in her mind before settling into a simple harmony. And with that, Ethan Fawcett found his most steadfast friend in the twenty-four-year-old quiet, devout Izzy Bianco.

14.

LATE THAT AFTERNOON, AFTER THE GROUP HAD RETURNED from the first day's ride, Travis called an emergency meeting in his hotel room to decide what to do about Ethan Fawcett and his "sons."

The room Travis and Ben were sharing was a mess, luxury sabotaged. The chintz-covered armchairs and snow-white comforters were strewn with bike gear, shoes, and T-shirts stamped with sayings on the back—"It's pronounced broo-SKETT-ah" on one and "I'm not yelling. I'm Italian!" on another.

Izzy found a clear space to sit on one of the beds. Chiara sat primly on the side of a chair. Ben stationed himself near her. Travis stood against a wall, twirling his phone in one hand and holding a water bottle in the other. He told them he'd sent an email to Hill and Dale headquarters in Austin and was waiting to hear back. It was still early there.

"What do you think they'll say?" Izzy asked.

"No clue," he answered, flipping the top of the water bottle on and off with his thumb. "He paid for all three of them. Full price."

"That's so out there," Ben said. Then he cleared his throat. "Well, I got an earful from the Seattle couple. The Beans."

Guests' bags were so often a perfect fit with their personalities. And the guides came to know each piece of luggage well, as they moved every piece of it to each new destination and placed the bags in each guest's room. Every brand of bag became a nickname.

"His bag is dark blue and hers is green," Ben said. "Navy and Lima Bean." Ben was chuckling. Travis laughed too. Even Izzy found herself smiling. Chiara looked confused.

"The Beans are complainers?" Travis asked.

"Big time," Ben replied. "Well, I don't know about the wife, but definitely the husband. He said he couldn't believe we'd let someone bring Bert and Ernie on a high-end bike trip. Austin will hear from him, for sure."

The Beans were traveling with a friend, a Microsoft engineer who'd brought one small backpack for the entire week. North Face. Apparently, North Face was very competitive with himself, determined to average sixty miles a day, even if it meant doing an extra loop twice. That morning, North Face had weighted his bike down with extra water bottles so he wouldn't have to stop. At lunch he sat with his friends but kept his head bent over his phone.

"Anyone else?" Travis asked, looking at Izzy and Chiara.

Izzy mentioned another couple, from New York.

"Oh, the Tumis," Travis said.

As they'd set off for the day, an athletic-looking man in his late seventies had rolled up to Ethan Fawcett, pointed to the bike trailer, and said, "Well, you won't have to worry about those kids whining." The comment had elicited a blank stare from Ethan, which made Izzy hope he hadn't heard it.

"Just to be clear," Ben said, "there's another set of Tumis."

"Right. The Tumis from Dallas," Travis said. "Tumi Twos."

"Oh yeah," Ben replied. "But the one from New York, Mr. Tumi One. He's a total blurter."

"What's his actual name?" Travis asked.

"Chauncey White. He's benign, though," Ben said. "He always says what's on his mind. His wife just rolls her eyes. Bet those two have been together for a hundred years."

"But here's the thing," Ben said. "For every harmless blurter like that, we're going to have four or five people like Mr. Bean feeling weirded out and pissed off."

"How'd it go today with . . . ?"

"Eagle," Ben said. "I handled his bag today. It's an Eagle Creek. And I don't want to know what's in there. It could be the rest of his family."

Izzy glared at him.

"Jesus, Izzy, lighten up," Ben said.

Ignoring Ben, Travis turned to Izzy. "How'd it go with Eagle today?" he asked her, as if inquiring about Izzy's time on a distant shore.

She was measured in her description. "It went well," she said. "He's shy. And sweet."

"Are you down with being the guy's minder until we figure out what to do?"

"Of course." Even as she said this, Izzy knew that she already was.

That morning, while Travis had delivered the daily route rap, Izzy had noticed Ethan Fawcett struggling with his tandem trailer and helped him attach it to the back of his bike. It was custom-built, narrow, and streamlined with a universal bike hitch, a special hinge, and reflectors on all sides, heavily waterproofed and designed to remain upright even if the bike tipped over. She could tell he was proud of it.

"I rode with him most of the day," she said. "He's nice. I like him."

She would be more forthcoming when she FaceTimed with Gus the next morning. Easygoing, understated Gus, brimming with empathy. If anybody would understand, he would.

"We need to get downstairs," Travis said. "Izzy, if this AGC shows signs of being truly fried, you'll let me know right away?"

This got Ben's attention. "What would those signs be?" he asked. "When he comes to dinner tonight with his origami wife? And how are *we* supposed to know if he's insane or just deeply weird?"

Izzy, too, had to wonder about that.

Travis didn't answer Ben. Until that moment, they had been discussing this bizarre surprise to their week as if they had a true grasp on it, when in fact they all knew they were playacting at handling a crisis. Broken bones and lost bikers, yes—even the occasional guest who was so high-maintenance that Roger Hill sent out what came to be known as a RogerGram, essentially telling the guest not to return on future trips. One couple had received a RogerGram after a marital spat that marked their undoing. At the communal dinner table the first night, the husband had turned to the wife and barked, "You didn't pack my socks," to which she responded, "I want a divorce." They had stayed through the week, making everyone so uncomfortable that one guest, recently divorced and traveling solo, demanded her money back, writing to the company, "If I'd wanted to relive that nightmare, I could have stayed home and stayed married." She got a full refund.

Travis's phone buzzed and he looked down at the incoming number. "It's Austin. Why don't you guys go down to the reception? I'll catch up with you."

When the get-to-know-you champagne reception got started in the hotel's elegant inner courtyard, Ethan Fawcett wasn't there, and Izzy doubted he would appear. The week's group numbered fifteen. They had been preparing for seventeen before realizing that Ethan Fawcett's children wouldn't need much in the way of food, guidance, or the usual Hill and Dale babysitting. All were Americans except one family of four from Australia—the two kids were in their late teens. They were the Monos. Ben was particularly taken with the Monos' bags, made in Australia, pricey rugged cases of polycarbonate with sturdy aluminum telescope handles and Japanese-made wheels. "Wheeling those things is better than sex," he had announced to the others that morning. The four Monos were fitness fanatics; the parents and their teenaged son and daughter were uncomplaining people whose default setting was a relaxed smile.

Chauncey and Annette White—the Tumi Ones—an older couple, both tall and ropy, were surveying the appetizer spread. "Hello, Izzy!" Chauncey fairly bellowed when he saw her. "You know, I was just telling Annette that you've got that same

fidgeting-with-your-jewelry habit that she has. When I'm annoying her, she starts fiddling with her wedding ring. That's her tell."

Annette glowered at him in mock annoyance, held up her
hand, and gave her ring a back-and-forth twist. Izzy laughed.
"And when she's in adoration mode, she goes for her necklace.
That's when I know she idolizes me."

Annette winked at Izzy and wandered away to say hello to new
friends, a group of four from Dallas—the Tumi Twos and the
Travelpros.

Chauncey watched his wife admiringly as she clinked glasses
with the Texans, then turned back to Izzy. He took a bite of cracker
and cheese and cupped his hand to his mouth as if sharing a secret.
"Hey, kiddo, I saw you out there riding with the guy with the
paper kids today. What's his name?" The word *paper* propelled bits
of food from his mouth. Izzy tried not to flinch. Everybody was
vaccinated and had been tested just before the trip.

"Ethan," Izzy said.

"Ethan, right. It was nice of you to ride with him." Then he
paused. "You're a giver, aren't you?"

Izzy shrugged shyly. She wasn't sure what to say. She hoped
Chauncey didn't really want an answer from her. She'd been called
a giver before—and not always as a compliment. Gus sometimes
said he thought she might be too much of one, so busy caring
about total strangers that she didn't have much left for herself. Or
for him.

But forbearance was a key marching order at Hill and Dale.
Izzy had understood this after her first and only conversation with
Roger Hill a few months earlier.

Gus had recommended Izzy for a job as a guide, and when she
went to Austin for the interview, Roger Hill himself asked to

meet with her. The meeting took place in his office, a glassed space no larger than any of the others that lined the north wall of the building, all with views up Congress Street to the Texas Capitol.

Hill's craggy face betrayed years of cycling around Texas hill country, blazing sun and big sky everywhere. He was in his forties. A lone piece of paper lay on his desk: her résumé looking puny and unimpressive.

"So you're the one who got stuck in Turin for a year," he said. "I've heard about you."

She laughed. "Nine months, actually. It was supposed to be six weeks."

"There are worse places to sit out a pandemic," he said. "I did love watching those videos of the famous Italian singers belting out arias from their balconies."

Izzy laughed. "I know, right? One of them lived in the building next door."

"That must have been a treat for you," he said. Then he sighed quietly and drifted somewhere else for a few seconds. She waited, wondering where the interview would go from there.

He continued. "Tell me a little bit about that experience in Italy."

"Well, since it was a six-week retreat—"

"A spiritual retreat?"

"Yes, but not really meditation, and definitely not silent." She explained that it had started out as a retreat for young people to engage in communal liturgical study by taking turns reading entire sections of the Bible aloud.

"Just reading it?"

"The purpose was to understand the Bible's immersive quality."

"Oh. It's not the most immersive reading I can think of, with all those *begat*s."

She laughed. "I was doing it partly out of curiosity. I did my senior thesis on intentional communities. And I'm Catholic, so the religious part interested me. . . ."

He was looking at her résumé. "So you were more of a participant observer?"

"Yes," she said. "And then when we got stuck there, we just kept going, until we had gone through the Old Testament, the New Testament, and all the gnostic gospels for good measure." Hill laughed at that. "My father said, 'You'll definitely find out who you are.'"

"And have you made progress with that?"

Izzy just smiled and shrugged. "I guess. But it was definitely hard being away from my family."

She stopped there. She didn't want to tell him about her grandmother, her precious Pearl, who had died alone in a hospital ICU early in the pandemic because no visitors were allowed, and her anguished mother, who had sobbed inconsolably to Izzy on the phone until Izzy's father took the phone from her. No, there would be no sharing of that kind with Roger Hill. "But I coped," she added.

"Do you think you're ready to be away from your family for long stretches again?"

"I'm two years out of college. I've gotten used to my independence, and I love biking. From what Gus tells me, I'd love to spend my summer doing this, especially in Italy."

Next: "How did those nine months in Italy change you?"

The question might have been rote, drawn from an interviewing template, but Hill's tone was one of genuine interest.

Izzy sat quietly for a moment. "It made me more wide-awake than I've ever been," she said. "If that makes sense."

He nodded. "Have you heard of Spirit Rock?"

Izzy shook her head.

Roger Hill told her of spending a week in his twenties in silent retreat at a place called Spirit Rock in California. "I didn't mind the silent part, though mealtimes were unbearable. The sound of everyone chewing was deafening." Izzy nodded, laughing.

"And what do you think you might want to do with the rest of your life?" Hill glanced at the résumé in front of him.

Izzy smiled. "I still don't really know," she told him. "Graduate school?"

Roger Hill leaned back in his chair, propped an elbow on each of the arms, and interlaced his fingers. He took in a breath and looked like he was getting ready to ask her another question. Just then, his administrative assistant poked his head in the door. "Megan's trying to reach you."

"Thanks," Roger Hill said. He rose from his chair, walked around the desk, and shook Izzy's hand. "I'm going to have to thank Gus for bringing you to us. He's one of our best, with us through thick and thin." Izzy knew what he meant about Gus. "A reference from him is all it takes for me to know I'm going to like someone. But now I can definitely say we'll be lucky to have you in the Hill and Dale family." Three weeks later she was in Italy, guiding her first group.

Gus had already ridden many of the Italy routes, and as a senior guide he went to Italy to help Travis do dry runs with the new hires, Izzy included, which had given them a solid week together before Gus left for California to lead a trip through Yosemite.

"I love this about you," Gus said one night as they lay in bed, Izzy's head resting on his chest. Gus was twirling the chain with the delicate gold cross around his index finger. When Izzy's grandmother had died, she'd bequeathed it to Izzy, along with her own grandmother's silver and peridot rosary, which Izzy's great-grandmother had herself inherited somewhere along the way.

Izzy and Gus had started out as cycling buddies their sophomore year in college in Ohio. Then they hooked up during a weekend biking trip with a group of friends. They both feared that sex might ruin their friendship, but it seemed only to deepen it. Within a few weeks, they'd placed themselves in the official category of dating. Gus was the one to push for exclusivity, so deeply did the lanky, fair-haired boy from the Ohio cornfields fall in love with the sincere, olive-complected Italian American girl from Brooklyn.

At first, she was quiet about her religion around Gus, who was avowedly agnostic. But Gus didn't shy away from it. If anything, he wanted to find out all he could. They began asking questions friends don't ask of each other but lovers do, and one Saturday morning as they lay in bed in his dorm room, he tugged gently at her cross. "Do you pray?" he asked.

Izzy told him she loved to pray and that she had faith her prayers would land somewhere. She didn't engage in pie-in-the-sky prayer but pragmatic, highly targeted requests. She prayed that her little brother would score a perfect five on his AP history exam (answered). She prayed that the Mets bullpen would stay uninjured for the 2016 season (it did, and then some). Gus admired Izzy's devoutness and loved to tease her about her very concrete petitions to God. "You could make an app and call it e-Pray-Love, Izz." She laughed as she took his hand and threaded her fingers through his.

She told Gus everything: her school, San Domenico; Sister Genevieve, her favorite teacher; and something Sister G. once told her students: religion is meant to comfort the afflicted and afflict the comfortable.

"I like that," Gus said.

Her interview with Roger Hill was all it took to convince Izzy that writing the RogerGrams gave Hill no pleasure. But he was a successful businessman, and that meant making some tough decisions. Hill and Dale relied on having guests return year after year—and on word of mouth. Guests who were high-maintenance to the point of sparking a contagion of negativity could be bad for the bottom line. There was one solo guest, now part of company lore, who obsessively tallied up what Hill and Dale charged against his estimate of what the company paid the hotels and restaurants on each of its itineraries. By the end of the week, he managed to convince the others that the Hill and Dale markup on its costs was excessive, stirring up waves of resentment that reached all the way to Texas. He received a RogerGram.

From her single conversation with Roger Hill, Izzy guessed that he would have told her to persevere with Ethan Fawcett. So she wasn't surprised when Travis took her aside during the reception to say that the word from Austin was to muddle through, as long as he was harmless. At least that was Travis's takeaway from the call. Ethan Fawcett was a returning guest who had paid in full, not just for himself but for the cardboard boys. He—and they—were, in fact, All God's Children.

15.

WHEN IZZY ARRIVED IN THE BREAKFAST ROOM THE NEXT morning, Ethan was standing at a window, holding a pastry above his head, his neck craned as he examined the croissant against the light. Tommy and Sam were seated by themselves at a table for four. Other Hill and Dale guests sat scattered around the room. The two couples from Texas, on a group vacation, were already chattering away, and it was barely 7:30 a.m. Many eyes were discreetly on the boys. *Do people think that staring at the boys is okay because they aren't alive*, Izzy wondered, *but staring at Ethan isn't okay because he is?*

"Okay if I join you?" Izzy asked Ethan after he sat down at the table with the boys, the pastry on his plate.

"Sure," Ethan said, nodding at the empty chair.

He was undeniably cute. Behind his glasses were alert brown eyes, which seldom met hers. He was passing one palm across his head of thick brown hair in a contemplative way. She found herself wanting to know what he might be thinking.

The boys were covered head to toe in Gore-Tex hooded rain jackets and waterproof pants. The outerwear engulfed them. So expertly had Ethan clad them, it was almost impossible to tell them apart from real kids.

Izzy had her marching orders. She was to remain with Ethan Fawcett as much as possible; she needed to ride with him without making it seem like she was his designated minder. What a week this promised to be, and it was only Day Two!

Simply put, Izzy didn't know what to say to Ethan. Nor, apparently, did he have a clue what to say to her. She had ridden with him the previous day, directly behind the trailer. It was all very awkward, with conversational fits and starts. She did most of the starting, but everything she tried had been a dead end. Small talk didn't seem to be his thing. He stayed quiet most of the time, which meant she did too.

As the day went on, Izzy guessed that Ethan Fawcett wasn't simply averse to small talk but was deathly afraid of conversation of any kind. This was far from unusual these days. In college Izzy had gone to a guest lecture by a sociologist who studied human conversation. In her talk, the professor said that people wore headphones and overused email because of a growing fear of actual conversation, because conversations could so easily veer off the rails. She called it the Goldilocks effect: we want to keep others at a comfortable distance—not too close, not too far, just right—so that we can stay in control. Hill and Dale requested that groups traveling together remain as podded as possible, especially during meals, when masks weren't an option. Still, the human need to socialize outweighed concern over the diminishing threat of the virus. Through this, her first summer of Hill and Dale bike trips, Izzy had grown increasingly fascinated by the way conversations among guests went from being stilted and cautious to familiar and jocular as the week wore on. She sometimes played a little game with herself, guessing which guests would bond over the course of the week. But Ethan Fawcett's discomfort when it came to open-ended conversation struck Izzy as a symptom of something more extreme than what most people experienced.

Out of the corner of her eye, Izzy saw Chauncey the Blurter approaching their table. Sure enough, within seconds, there he loomed, in full biking gear, cleats and all.

"Good morning!" Izzy said cheerfully.

"Top o' the morning to you!" Chauncey said. He had the *New York Times* International Edition tucked under his arm and was balancing a cup of coffee in each hand. As he bowed to Izzy, the bone china cups tinkled against their saucers. "And how are these two rascals doing this morning?" he asked, nodding in the direction of Tommy and Sam.

Chauncey didn't wait for an answer—thank goodness, Izzy thought—and launched into his next topic.

"My princess bride is taking breakfast in bed this morning, and she's sent me out to inquire as to timing and route options."

"Ben will be doing the route rap at nine on the side of the building where the bikes are," Izzy said. "Just go out the main entrance and it's on the left. There's an optional loop before lunch for people who want to ride longer. I'd recommend getting more riding in today and tomorrow because Wednesday's supposed to be really hot."

"Thank you, my dear! I'll deliver that news."

Chauncey bowed again and backed away a dozen feet as if taking leave of Queen Elizabeth. Izzy was starting to like Chauncey.

She felt herself beginning to relax, but Chauncey had one last blurt in him. It could no more remain unexpressed than the steam beneath Old Faithful. "You know, Ethan, there are a lot of sports stadiums that could use the boys to fill their seats!" Izzy squirmed, and Ethan appeared puzzled. Before Ethan could reply, Chauncey had turned and left.

Ethan looked at the boys and said something in a language that Izzy couldn't make out. Hungarian? Russian? It was the first time she'd heard him speak directly to them. Maybe he was feeling more comfortable with her.

Ethan turned to her and spoke. "That pre-lunch loop is really beautiful," he said. "There's a whole row of houses painted with murals."

"You've done your research!" Izzy said.

"I've done this trip before."

"Really?" she said. "This exact trip?" He nodded.

This was a data point about Ethan Fawcett that Travis hadn't mentioned. Was it possible that Travis didn't know?

"That's great that you've already done this trip!" Izzy said. "It must feel pretty different after Covid."

And then nothing. Another conversational dead end.

Ethan stood and gathered the boys from their seats, put them into a backpack harness built for holding children, and hoisted it onto his back.

"I'll see you out there," she said.

"Okay," he replied. People stared as he left the room.

At 8:36, Izzy was brushing her teeth when a text came in from Travis: "The Eagle's flown. Pls go find him." Two minutes later she was on her bike, clipped in, and racing up the road. Ethan Fawcett was certain to be going fast on that e-bike. Guests were encouraged to start out for the day as soon as they were ready and to ride at their own pace. Still, Izzy thought, Ethan Fawcett would take some watching.

She was hugely relieved when she rounded a corner and saw the back of the trailer a few hundred yards ahead. "Ethan!" she called out. He didn't stop. Maybe he hadn't heard her.

The long uphill stretch was the most difficult of the morning. She shifted into a low gear, stood up on her bike, and pedaled with all the torque her legs could supply.

When she was a hundred feet or so behind the trailer, she called out again. This time, Ethan looked around and stopped to wait. When she caught up, she stopped too.

"I think that was the hardest hill of the day," she said, hoping her words concealed her heavy panting. He was smiling. He reached over and patted the front of his handlebars, as an equestrian might stroke a horse's withers. "This e-bike is doing a great job," he said.

"I'm so glad to hear that," Izzy said. "And we have a nice downhill for the next two kilometers."

"Is the road smooth?" he asked.

"I think so."

"Just to be safe," he said, and he jumped off his bike. "Would you mind holding my bike for a minute?"

Izzy held the e-bike steady while Ethan unzipped the trailer and gave each boy's seat belt a reassuring tug.

The gesture made Izzy think of her grandmother. If they were on the subway or a bus together, her grandmother always made sure Izzy was seated or holding on to something. Izzy patted her pocket for her grandmother's letter; feeling it there reminded her that she needed to find just the right mailbox.

16.

ITALY WAS BURNING UP. BY 9:00 A.M., THE TEMPERATURE was in the low hundreds. The air was motionless under the fervid sky, the grapevines drooping in a heavy sulk.

Earlier that morning during the pre-ride team huddle, Travis had taken Izzy aside to tell her it was Ethan Fawcett's birthday. The H&D database flagged guests celebrating birthdays or other special occasions. The company's tradition was to tie a custom-printed balloon to the bicycle of the birthday guest and have it waiting that morning—always a fun surprise. Travis pulled out the balloon: HAPPY BIRTHDAY, ETHAN! He shook his head. "What if this sends him off the deep end? How awkward would that be? Are we all going to sing for this nutcase? And what if the kids are allergic to latex!" He tossed the balloon back into the van.

The unrelenting heat and a series of steep climbs through the morning of the fourth day conspired to make the guests miserable. Even the strongest riders were having a rough time. Ben rode with the group and cajoled people to persevere, doling out *attaboy*s like they were water bottles. Only North Face seemed to be unaffected by the temperature, speeding ahead then looping back to rejoin the Beans.

Chauncey and Annette brought up the rear, Chauncey gamely riding behind his wife.

"Hon, you'd do a lot better if you changed your gears more often," he called out to her.

"I'll get you for this," she panted back at him. "Next year, Scandinavia, where it's flat and cool! Or better yet, a cruise on the Rhine!"

"PMA!" Chauncey replied.

"That *is* a positive mental attitude!" Annette shouted back at her husband.

Travis and Chiara stationed themselves at the top of the steepest hill of the day, cheering the riders on and splashing them with ice water as they rode past. A few kept riding but many stopped to catch their breath and take a drink.

Izzy wanted to stop too but she stayed with Ethan, who shot straight past the group. As she cycled on, out of the corner of her eye she saw Travis's head turn in the direction of the receding sight of Ethan and the trailer.

After another kilometer or two, Izzy's head was pounding. Her water bottle was empty. She needed a break. She saw on her Garmin that they were approaching Rutte, a tiny dot of a town on the map. She got ahead of Ethan and, spotting a bar across a small piazza, she stopped her bike and waited for him. When he pulled up, she asked, "Ethan, do you mind if we get something cold to drink here?"

"Sure, no problem," Ethan said. When he removed his eyeglasses to wipe his face, Izzy took further note of his appearance.

The glasses obscured long lashes, thick dark eyebrows, and chiseled cheekbones. He had a scruff of beard coming on, a tad darker than his brown hair. Yet he carried himself as if he possessed no knowledge of his looks, not an ounce of swagger.

In repose, Ethan's face was calm and kind, if occasionally fretful. But in an instant, when the village church bell rang, he seemed distracted, and his mouth fixed into a thin, tight line.

"Can I treat you to a *shakerato*?" Izzy asked Ethan.

"A what?"

"A *caffè shakerato*. It's Italy's version of iced coffee. It's a shot of espresso with ice cubes, shaken up like a cocktail. There's a syrup in there, too, but I don't know what it is."

Ethan seemed intrigued. "Sure," he said.

They walked their bikes across the deserted square. The bar appeared to be the only establishment that was open. Outside was a handwritten sign: *"Per piacere, solo clienti vaccinati."* Only vaccinated customers, please.

"I'll be right back," Izzy told Ethan.

As soon as Izzy scanned her QR code and heard a confirmation chime from the café's scanner, the barista called out to her from behind the bar. *"Buongiorno!"*

Inside the café, behind the bar, stood the establishment's centerpiece: a large gleaming espresso machine. No matter how impoverished an Italian town might be, there would always be money for a high-end espresso machine. Izzy took in the colorful display of Mentos for sale, the sugar bowl in the shape of a giant demitasse, a plastic wall clock that said "Grand Central Terminal," the glistening copper that ran the length of the counter. A lone cake dotted with whole hazelnuts was on display on the counter, on a pedestal under a glass cake dome. A quarter of the cake was gone. A housefly was crawling up the inside of the dome, trapped.

Izzy leaned on the counter and ordered the drinks, relishing the contact of her bare arms with the cool metal. The barman was tall and wiry, his elongated face layered with folds like a dried fig. There was no telling his age. Taped to the counter was a printed sign bearing the slogan that had popped up on posters all over Italy in the past two years: *Andrà tutto bene.* Everything will be all right. When she emerged from the café, a glass in each hand, she saw Ethan bent over the trailer, pulling out his water bottle. "Better?" he said to the boys. When he straightened up, Izzy handed him a glass. He took a sip. He had never tasted anything so delicious, he told her. He finished it in three large swallows. When Izzy looked at his face, she was surprised to see that he wore a wistful look and was gazing around the square as if in search of something. He seemed to have forgotten she was there.

The barista came outside to retrieve their empty glasses and clicked his tongue in admiration of their fortitude.

"*Fa un caldo boia,*" he said.

"*Sì, sì,*" Izzy replied. She turned to Ethan. "The heat is an executioner."

"I noticed." Ethan's bittersweet smile had turned into a lopsided grin. As they started walking their bikes across the square toward the road, Ethan surprised Izzy by speaking. "I don't remember this café, but it looks like it's been here forever."

A bench they had passed on their way toward the bar was now occupied by what looked like an elderly couple. But as they drew nearer they could see that they were actually two life-size cloth figures plump with stuffing. A man and a woman. Both had gray hair made of yarn. Their eyes were flat black buttons, their lips red yarn. The woman doll was dressed in a shapeless cotton shift with a floral print that reminded Izzy of the lightweight dresses her grandmother used to wear on hot summer days. Her legs were made of material that looked like linen. Her bench-mate was wearing a fedora, angled down over the upper third of his face. Both wore close-toed sandals. Their feet didn't reach the ground.

Izzy hoped Ethan didn't see her staring. But when she glanced over at him, she saw that he had slowed almost to a standstill. He was looking at the dolls too.

A loud clattering made both of them look up. Approaching from across the blank piazza was a woman pulling a jumbo wagon made of steel mesh. It was filled with a dozen or so dolls similar to those on the bench. The woman's eyes were fixed on Izzy and Ethan.

"*Buongiorno*," Izzy said to the woman as she drew closer. The woman was short, stout, and full-breasted. A large crucifix hung around her neck. Like the doll on the bench, she was wearing a cotton shift with bright-green plastic buttons down the front. The last button was undone. The dress fell to just below her knees. Izzy introduced herself and Ethan, who nodded and gave the woman a shy *ciao*. Izzy asked the woman about the dolls in the wagon, which were seated, upright and alert, as if being treated to a special outing. The woman peered into the trailer at the boys. What she saw must have agreed with her, because she began speaking quickly, too quickly for Izzy to translate seamlessly.

"Her name is Signora Fiore," Izzy said. "I already made a gaffe. I asked her if the dolls are hers, and she said they are not dolls. They are cloth people. *Gente di stoffa*." When the woman heard this, she nodded vigorously. "*Sì. Gente di stoffa*," she said, and she kept talking.

"Signora Fiore makes the cloth people, but they belong to the community. To everyone."

Izzy was trying to formulate a polite way of asking Signora Fiore why she made the cloth people when the woman supplied the answer. "She says this town is known as a 'village at the edge.'" Izzy studied Signora Fiore's crosshatched face as she translated her words. "There are many of these villages around Italy. First the young people moved to the cities. They left the elderly—'the ancients,' they call them—behind. Then the ancients died." Signora Fiore was shaking her head as she surveyed the empty square. "Then the pandemic came and even more of the older people died. This village used to have five hundred people. Now there are forty-five. Signora Fiore is sixty-five and she's one of the oldest people in the village now."

Signora Fiore paused and mumbled something to the couple on the bench, then turned back to Izzy, who translated for Ethan. "These are Signor and Signora Sartore. Signor Sartore died first, and then his wife died a few days later. The Sartores were the tailors in town, she says." Ethan looked confused. "*Sartore* means *tailor*," Izzy explained. Signora Fiore tugged at a button on her dress and pantomimed the pulling of needle and thread. She smiled at the two Americans, revealing blank spots on either side of her mouth where teeth were missing. "She just said something about her name, which means *flower*," Izzy said. "But she isn't a—"

Before Izzy could finish Signora Fiore's sentence, the woman and her wagon were back in motion. Izzy and Ethan followed her to a nearby pair of benches, both empty, mercifully shaded under a red chestnut. As if suddenly reminded of something urgent, Signora Fiore bent her wide frame over the wagon, plucked out one of the dolls, and placed it on the bench. "This is Signora

Ricci," Izzy translated. Signora Fiore sat down beside the doll, then pointed to the adjacent bench, signaling for Izzy and Ethan to join her. "Signora Fiore and Signora Ricci were best friends from grade school," Izzy translated. "And this was their favorite place to meet and sit. Now Signora Ricci lives in the village again. Signora Ricci still wears her own clothes. Most of the cloth people do."

Izzy said something to Signora Fiore, then turned to Ethan as the woman answered. "I asked her if seeing the figure of her close friend made her sad now, and she is telling me no."

Ethan interrupted. "It doesn't make her sad because now she can come and sit down with her friend and talk to her whenever she wants to," he suggested. Izzy smiled. Signora Fiore was listening politely and smiling. In a nod to decorum, she pulled at the hem of Signora Ricci's dress to cover her friend's lumpy knees, then kept talking. "Signora Fiore was born and raised here," Izzy said. "When people started dying in the village, the emptiness gave her a huge canvas to work with. She has always liked to sew. So last year, she started sewing the cloth people. She's made more than a hundred of them. They are real people. People who died."

The bells of the church rang, and a solitary woman in a black shawl left the church and crossed the piazza. Signora Fiore was still talking. "The people who died are *gli spariti*." Izzy stopped, unsure how to translate this. "*Gli spariti*, they're called," she said. "The vanished."

"The vanished?" Ethan asked. Izzy nodded. Signora Fiore was still talking. "Some of the cloth people aren't people who died. Like Signora Fiore's own children. They live in Milan. Her daughter is a doctor. Her son owns a furniture store. She has sewn them because she doesn't know when she'll see them again."

As Signora Fiore was speaking, Izzy flashed on her own neighborhood in Brooklyn, also now something of a ghost town. As Izzy's relatives on the Bianco side always told the story, starting in the 1930s, Mafia bosses installed their grandmothers in the ten-block area, making Carroll Gardens one of the safest neighborhoods in the five boroughs. Izzy never asked her family if they, too, fit into that category, but she suspected they did. On long summer nights, Italian grandmothers sat outside on their stoops, in billowy cotton dresses not unlike those on the cloth dolls. Over the years, the grandmothers died. *Gli spariti.* Their houses were sold to young couples with babies and jogging strollers. The neighborhood was infused with cold-brew coffee and yoga studios, but its stories had been scrubbed away. Only the Biancos remained to remember them. For as long as Izzy could remember, her grandmother had lived with them, a point of pride for Izzy through her childhood. Now the Bianco family brownstone on President Street was a ruin of a place compared to others on the block, or in the entire neighborhood, for that matter. People who had known Carroll Gardens as it once was found it hard not to lament the change.

During the months Izzy was stranded in Turin, her family told her, the street had come back to life. Kids learning from home turned that block of President Street, now free of cars, into a playground, with baseball mitts and skateboard ramps and chalk-drawn hopscotch grids. Through the summer, at dusk, people were back on their stoops. But when the schools reopened, the traffic returned, and the street died all over again, not gradually this time, but all at once, as if it were in a hurry to blot out a bad dream.

Izzy admired Signora Fiore for creating this facsimile of a peopled town.

"And why does she have some of the cloth people in her wagon?" Ethan asked. This was the first question Izzy had heard Ethan ask of anyone, about anything.

Izzy was so surprised to hear him express curiosity that she forgot to translate for Signora Fiore and sat waiting for a reply. Ethan and the woman were staring at Izzy expectantly.

"Sorry! I spaced out," Izzy said to Ethan, and she asked the question in Italian. "She spends a couple of hours every day distributing them around town," she told Ethan, turning to Signora Fiore to make sure that was right.

"*Tutti i giorni?*"

"*Sì, sì. Ogni giorno.*"

Izzy continued. "She brings them out for the day and puts them in their favorite spots around the village. Her husband helps her most days, but he complained this morning that it's too hot to go outside. He got very sick last year, so she doesn't make him do too much. The people she takes out with her wagon are just the ones that like to be outside. Some stay inside all the time." The effort it took to keep up with Signora Fiore and make her words understood to Ethan, under the soul-crushing heat, was causing Izzy's eyes to ache.

Signora Fiore pointed to another doll in the wagon, dressed in a sleeveless cotton dress with a geometric print that was identical to Signora Fiore's, as well as a pinafore with two large front pockets. "This is her sister, Fenisia, who died when she was only fifty-eight. Fenisia was a schoolteacher. The school here was open until three years ago. It closed because there weren't enough students."

Ethan was nodding, but Izzy was confused. "You mean it closed even before the pandemic?" she asked Signora Fiore. "*Sì. Sì*," the woman said.

"Young people with children were already leaving for the big cities," Izzy translated, "and the pandemic was the final blow."

Signora Fiore got up and motioned to them to follow her. Izzy anxiously checked the time on her phone. She was coming perilously close to being late for her lunch-prep duties. Before she could say anything, Ethan was in motion, walking his bike and the boys' trailer behind the clackety-clack of Signora Fiore's wagon as it traversed the cobbled pavement. A shimmer of heat danced across the square.

The dolls bounced up and down with each turn of the wheels, as rhythmic as Clydesdale hooves. "A happy bunch," Ethan remarked to Izzy. He looked relaxed, not at all discomfited to be pushing a bike that pulled two cardboard kids, trailing after a stranger pulling a wagon filled with life-size dolls. Then again, why would he be? For three days Izzy had been asking, *How can he be so at home in his delusion?* Now it was Izzy who was growing unsure of her footing in this Italian village. She now questioned her assumption that people who imbue non-people with people-like traits were most decidedly out of balance. She was beginning to see Signora Fiore's cloth people as the woman herself did, and even to view Tommy and Sam as more—far more, in fact—than cardboard. For as this unlikely parade made its way through the deserted little town, its presence seemed as unremarkable as daylight.

Signora Fiore led them down a narrow side street to a low building in the middle of the block. *La Scuola Elementare del Comune di Rutte* was painted on the stucco above the door in faded red letters. "This is the elementary school that shut down. Signora Fiore was a pupil here, and her own children were too." As she spoke, Signora Fiore lifted Fenisia from the wagon. A piece of white chalk tumbled out of one of the pockets of Fenisia's pinafore and lodged between two cobblestones; Signora Fiore didn't seem to notice. Izzy picked it up, but before she could put it back in the pocket, Signore Fiore had tucked her sister under her plump arm.

Ethan and Izzy propped their bikes against the shaded building. Signora Fiore turned the rusted handle and shoved the door open with her shoulder. Once inside, she switched on the light to reveal a dozen or so desks placed in three rows, all facing the front of the room. At each desk sat a cloth child, most of them slightly canted to one side. Ethan and Izzy stood for a moment taking the scene in.

But then Ethan did something Izzy found unexpected. He bent over a cloth boy seated near the door where they had entered. A seam on one of the arms had come undone, and some white cotton stuffing bulged out. Izzy watched as Ethan gently pushed it back in, then held the cloth boy's lifeless hand in his palm and lifted it an inch or two, as if reading its weight. Then he frowned and let it drop.

Signora Fiore was shuffling to the front of the room, where she placed her sister into the chair behind the teacher's desk, talking all the while. "She wanted her sister to be able to teach again, so she sewed these students," Izzy translated for Ethan. "Signora Fiore says her daughter and son send clothes their children have outgrown and she uses them for the schoolchildren. The children stay at the school, but she brings Fenisia home with her at the end of the school day so she won't get too lonely."

Izzy walked over and knelt next to the teacher, surveying the view of the entire class from Fenisia's perspective. As she dropped the chalk she'd been holding back into Fenisia's pinafore pocket, she took in the doll's face. There was something about it—the round chin, the soft folds of cloth—that reminded her of her grandmother. She felt the letter in her pocket. "Fenisia," she whispered. "Make sure this gets to Pearl." She pulled the envelope from her own pocket and slipped it into the doll's.

She looked up and caught Ethan's eye. "I'll meet you back outside," he said; then he turned and left.

Once they were all outside again, they stood for a moment in the generous shade of the building. "This town is lucky to have you," Ethan said to Signora Fiore.

Izzy looked at Ethan. "Do you mean the town is fortunate to have her here as God's healer and sew all the cloth people to stand in for the ones who are gone?"

He looked surprised. "Maybe," he said.

Izzy smiled and translated this for Signora Fiore. She expected the woman to be pleased by the compliment. But the woman's face darkened, and her kindly aspect disappeared. "*Fortunata?*" Signora Fiore said. She gestured toward the building, toward the ghost of her sister. "*Vivo ma sono condannata a questo.*" She was telling them that she was living, but the town was not fortunate, she was not fortunate. Her tone was at once rote and rhythmic, resembling a chant. Izzy was having trouble understanding everything she was saying. She comprehended an intermittent word or phrase. God. Humble. Light. Darkness. Now the woman was craning her neck to the sky, ablaze with the midday sun. "There is no such thing as the fortunate," Signora Fiore said.

The woman's dark turn startled Izzy, who thought Italians to be if not blasé then shrug-of-the-shoulders fatalistic about God's intentions, believing he was in control of even the most random events.

Ethan had one arm across his torso, propping up his elbow, his fist under his chin. He was looking off somewhere, not quite present. Something told Izzy not to translate any of what Signora Fiore had just said.

Before Izzy could speak again, Signora Fiore and her wagon were on the move, heading back toward the town square. Back at Signora Ricci's bench, Signora Fiore seated herself next to her old friend with a heavy sigh and spoke to Izzy. "She needs to excuse herself," Izzy told Ethan. "She has to go home to get more cloth people to distribute around the village, and without her husband's help, the job will take longer than usual." Signora Fiore repeated what she'd already told them about her husband's illness and recovery. Izzy thanked her for her time and Ethan said, "Yes, thank you."

"It's too hot for the children on a day like this," Signora Fiore said in a scolding tone directed at Ethan. "They need to be inside." Izzy didn't translate those last words. With that, Signora Fiore stood and waved goodbye to them, mumbling something to Signora Ricci that Izzy didn't catch.

Back on their bikes, Ethan pedaled in a contemplative pace in front of Izzy, the boys bumping along inside the trailer. They were so late for lunch they might miss it altogether, but Izzy didn't say anything.

"Did we just dream that?" Ethan asked.

"Maybe," Izzy said, laughing. Another question from Ethan Fawcett. *I think I'm making him happy*, she thought. She pedaled her bike alongside his on the empty road.

"What did you put in the teacher's pocket?" he asked. "At the school."

"A piece of chalk that fell out," Izzy said, glancing over at him. He didn't look convinced.

"It looked like a piece of paper," he said.

"It was a letter to my grandmother," she confessed.

"Your grandmother?"

"We've always written letters to each other. All my life. So I still write to her."

"Did she live in Italy?"

"She came from a small village in Italy. In the south," Izzy said. "But she lived with us in Brooklyn."

"She lived with you but you wrote letters to each other?"

"Yes, and our quote 'mailbox' was under a cushion on the couch in the living room." She couldn't believe she was telling Ethan this. She hadn't even told Gus about the "Dear Pearl" letters. "She died last year, and I couldn't get home because of Covid. So I've been mailing the letters from different places in Italy. I mailed that one from the sister's pocket."

"I'm sure she'll get it," he said. "What was her name?"

"Isabella, like me," Izzy said. "But I called her Pearl."

They rode in silence for a while; then Ethan said, "If we did dream that back there, it was a very nice dream."

"Yes," Izzy said. "It was." She found herself pedaling faster, so easily was her body producing energy. She was fairly soaring. She turned around, thinking she might have left Ethan behind. But there he was, pedaling right next to her. His e-bike gave him a more upright position than a regular bike to be sure, but he seemed to be sitting up much straighter in his seat than she'd seen him all week, riding at full mast.

They arrived for lunch on the patio of a rustic trattoria just as everyone was sitting down. Travis glared at Izzy from across the patio in silent rebuke for her tardiness. All she could manage in return was a wan smile and a slight shrug. Ben and Chiara stood at the buffet swatting flies away from the food.

Ethan had already filled his plate and sat down. Tommy and Sam were propped on either side of him. Travis came up to Izzy and pulled her aside.

"We have a problem," he said. Izzy looked over at Ethan, who was watching her, waiting for her to join him.

"Not that problem," he said. "The Beans are fighting. You missed the shouting."

"What about?" She scanned the patio for the Beans and saw they were seated at opposite ends of a long picnic table, eating in silence.

"He said something about her not changing gears correctly and she blew up."

"Oh geez."

"And North Face has been grousing about his bike. We've already traded it out once and he still isn't happy."

"Really?" she said. "These bikes are top quality. Who would do that?"

"A pinhead," he said. "Sorry to pull you away from Eagle, but you need to spend the afternoon riding with the Beans and North Face and applying your slow-burn-of-Izzy charm. Get Mr. Bean to cut his wife some slack. There are some serious hills this afternoon. And spend some time talking bike technology with North Face, even if you have to do some bullshitting."

"Sure," Izzy said. She looked over at Ethan, who now waved at her. She felt her heart sink.

• • • •

Dinner that night was outside in the hotel's courtyard under a huge trellis covered with grapevines. Ethan and the boys were nowhere to be seen.

The Beans and the Tumi Ones and North Face were already seated together, laughing loudly.

"I don't know what you did, but whatever it was, it worked," Travis said to Izzy as the guides fanned out to sit with different groups.

"I just gave both the Beans some tips on tackling the hills," she said. "And you were right about North Face. He just needed to get to know us as people. Now he loves his bike."

But Izzy couldn't get Ethan out of her head. The tragedy of his spending the evening of his birthday in self-imposed seclusion in his room was something she couldn't stop thinking about. As dessert was being served—an intensely rich chocolate torta—she asked one of the waiters if she might take the delicacy up to one of the guests who was celebrating his birthday. The waiter returned with a generous slice of the cake, ringed with *paste di meliga*, cornmeal shortbread cookies that were a specialty of the region.

Izzy met Chauncey and Annette White at the lobby elevators. Of course, Chauncey couldn't let the sight of the dessert go unremarked. "Just in case you get a midnight craving?" he asked.

"Well, actually, it's Ethan's birthday. I'm taking this to him." The couple surveyed the offering. The plate looked beautiful, with edible flowers atop the cake, the flank of cookies propped against it.

"Hah! I have a birthday poem I've written for him," Chauncey said. "I'll just dash up to our room and get it. What floor is he on?"

"Three," Izzy said.

"I'll meet you there!"

A birthday poem? "How did he know it was Ethan's birthday?" Izzy asked Annette, who was wearing a long-suffering smile.

"He didn't," she said. "He reads the same poem to everyone and claims he's written it just for them. He does some customizing on the fly. It's one of his things. You'll see."

Within minutes, the elevator opened on the third floor and Chauncey stepped out, a tattered, folded sheet of paper in his hand. Izzy knocked on Ethan Fawcett's door, suddenly doubting their plan. Perhaps he disliked surprises. But the wheels were already in motion.

Ethan opened the door a crack. "Happy birthday!" Chauncey bellowed. He and Annette broke into the birthday song, and Izzy joined in. A few doors along, people peered out of their rooms. By the end, as Annette and Chauncey were singing "And many mooooore" in practiced harmony, the people scattered along the hallway started clapping and saying "Happy birthday!" in various accents. Izzy was relieved to see both Beans standing in their doorway. Mrs. Bean was clapping, but Mr. Bean, already in his bathrobe, looked disgruntled, as if his wife had force-marched him out of their room.

Izzy was almost too frightened to look at Ethan, but when she did, she saw he had a wide smile on his face. Izzy immediately felt lighter. He didn't invite them in, but he stepped into the hallway, propping the door open with his foot. Izzy's relief was quickly overtaken by the heart-catching sight of the boys tucked into a bed in the alcove.

Izzy thrust the plate in his direction. "I have to warn you. There might be nut traces."

"That's okay," he said. "I'll eat it out here."

"What birthday is this, old chap?" Chauncey asked. "I'm guessing thirty-five."

"You're close," Ethan said. "Thirty-eight."

"How does it feel?" Annette asked.

"Just another birthday," Ethan replied.

"I've written you a poem, my man," Chauncey said with such gusto that Izzy came close to believing he'd written it in a burst of inspiration, maybe in the elevator. Ethan speared the cake and offered cookies to the others. Chauncey took two, chewed them quickly, and began to read:

> *It must feel pretty weird to turn thirty-eight,*
> *You simply can't imagine a more momentous fate.*

That part *must* have been made up on the spot. Annette chuckled. "Nice one, Chaunce," she said. Her husband cleared his throat and continued:

> *You're not thinking much about the money you've earned,*
> *But fretting about the chances you've spurned.*

> *Ethan, please take stock, think of the glory of roads chosen,*
> *Climbing mountains, swimming oceans, skating on lakes*
> *frozen,*
> *On this day, think of what will be written on your eternal*
> *scroll,*
> *And reflect on the good long shadow you're casting with*
> *your soul.*

Izzy was surprised by how fitting that bad poem seemed to be. When he was finished, Chauncey gave a little bow. Annette was smiling. She had clearly seen a version of this performance many times before—but, Izzy was sure, never in a situation quite like this.

Ethan handed the empty plate back to Izzy. "That was delicious. Thank you," he said. "And I really liked the poem."

"Happy birthday!" the three of them said in near unison. "Good night!"

17.

"WHAT DO YOU THINK MAKES ETHAN TICK?"

Izzy and Gus were FaceTiming one morning when Gus asked that question. It was nighttime for him in California, where he was leading his Yosemite trip. Now was their time, the time they carved out every day to talk—early in the morning for her and late at night for him. She told Gus about the impromptu birthday gathering at Ethan's door, and she was eager to tell him about Signora Fiore and the cloth people. Gus was the only person Izzy felt safe talking to about Ethan Fawcett, who had quickly become the main topic of their FaceTime conversations. Gus already knew about pretty much every aspect of Izzy's unusual week so far: about the way the other guides were keeping their distance from Ethan since that first awkward morning; about the stream of requests Ethan had sent to the Austin guest-experience staff, which had ended up on Travis's laptop a few hundred feet from Ethan's room; about other guests complaining to Travis and probably to Austin too.

Izzy told Gus about Ethan's small displays of thoughtfulness, like waiting for her at the top of hills after getting there first on his e-bike. They wondered how the boys had come into his life and whether he truly thought they were real. She told Gus she had gotten up the courage to ask Ethan about the mysterious Barb, who had come with him on this very trip a few years earlier, and that Ethan had said they were taking a break but didn't elaborate. "Sarah was on that trip," Gus said, referring to another guide whom he was riding with that week. "I asked her about Ethan. She said Barb was great."

But they hadn't yet addressed the central question: What makes Ethan Fawcett tick?

"I honestly don't know," Izzy said. "But I like him. There's something so—I don't know—so pure about him and his love for the boys."

"Are you the only one riding with them—" he stopped himself. "I mean him?"

"Yeah."

"What about meals?"

"He doesn't show up for breakfast anymore. Or dinner. At lunch it's me and him and the two boys. And sometimes the couple from New York. Chauncey and Annette. Chauncey's the blurter. But Chauncey gets Ethan. Or maybe he's just too oblivious to feel uncomfortable."

"How's Travis dealing with all of this?" Gus looked exhausted, his floppy hair sticking out in different directions from hours under a bike helmet. He and Travis had been on trips together, and Gus had a hard time imagining how Travis—whose veneer of chill could quickly crack if he was confronted with something out of his wheelhouse—might be dealing with the Ethan issue.

"Travis is taking a hands-off approach," she replied. "He's supposed to be in charge, but I think the whole Ethan situation is too much for him. He's kind of passed it off to me."

"I get that. But Izzy—" Now Gus's expression was almost stern. "Travis might be having a problem dealing with the problem. But Ethan *is* a problem."

Izzy was quiet. She felt defensive and a bit miffed. Gus filled in the silence, softening his tone. "I don't want to make you feel bad, but I'm worried this is classic Izzy. He's your wounded bird of the week, and somehow you think you're going to be able to save him. From where I sit . . . ."

"Thousands of miles and nine time zones away," Izzy reminded him. It came out edgier than she had intended.

"Right. Okay. But from here, it's seeming a lot like his problem is bigger than he is, which means it's a lot bigger than you are."

She scrapped her plan to tell Gus about Signora Fiore; she now felt uncomfortable telling him anything even vaguely strange or intimate.

"Is this guy good-looking?" Gus asked, suddenly changing tack.

Izzy felt her face grow hot. "C'mon Gus, he's old," she said. The fact that she couldn't admit that she found Ethan distractingly attractive made her feel defensive and strange.

"I'm not saying I'm going to save him," she said. "I'm just saying that we could all learn something from him. He's a teaching parable, a living, breathing definition of a parable."

"Which parable?"

"I'm not thinking of a specific one." She stopped and took a breath, unsure of herself. "I'd have to think about it. Maybe he's his own unique parable. My point is that parables are simple stories, but they aren't stories about things that are obvious, and their lessons aren't black-and-white. Parables point the finger at us. They force us to look inward. And if we don't, we're missing the point." Now she was preaching. She felt awful. It was their first real fight in nearly five years.

She thought she'd been paying attention to the time, but when she glanced at the top of her screen she saw it was already 7:55. If she didn't hurry, Ethan might start riding by himself again.

"I have to go," she said.

"Have a great ride today, Izz." Gus's palm swept across his camera. And he was gone.

She hadn't eaten breakfast and was hungry, but she rushed past the dining room and out the side door. Ben was just ending the route rap, and Izzy spotted Ethan and the boys at the top of the hotel's drive, waiting for her. Ethan bent to fiddle with Sam's safety strap. There was something tender in the gesture, in the way his hand rested for a moment on the boy's head afterward. The sight lifted her from her low mood.

The sky was dappled with clouds. It was the first day without a blazing, ceaseless sun. Each morning, Ethan had mentioned the clear sky, but today he said nothing about the weather, which made Izzy wonder: Was he getting more adventurous, or was he fretting quietly? As the morning wore on, the clouds grew darker, thickening above the hills. Still, it didn't rain.

Lunch was at a winery overlooking acres of vineyards stretched across undulating slopes, the meal accompanied by a leisurely wine tasting. Ethan politely shook his head each time the garrulous vintner offered to pour him a sip. Chauncey, seated on the other side of Izzy, leaned across her and said to Ethan, "That's what I call good modeling. Kids see their parents drinking in the middle of the day and there's your slippery slope."

Travis announced that the weather seemed to be changing and offered the daily post-lunch option of riding in the van back to the hotel. Izzy was certain that with even a slight chance of rain, Ethan would take the ride. But he didn't budge, and within a few minutes, Izzy, Ethan, and the boys set out for the afternoon stretch. After ten kilometers the wind kicked up and the sky turned a dark, forbidding gray. Izzy saw the first heavy drops fall on the pavement. Ethan pulled up the hood on the carriage to protect the boys from the moisture, which would work for a drizzle but not if it began to pour.

Izzy struggled to keep pace with Ethan. Once she reached his side, she said, "Let's stop at the next town and wait the rain out." She checked her Garmin. "It looks like there's one coming up in about a kilometer." Ethan's face wore an expression of distress. She heard him turn back and say something to the boys, and then he picked up speed.

A small sign on a rusted post told them they were entering Coazzolo, a town that appeared to consist of one restaurant (closed), a post office (also closed), and a church. Izzy was about to suggest they take shelter under the restaurant's deep awning when she noticed that the church door was open. "Ethan! Come back. Into the church!" It was raining so hard now—a wall of rain—she worried he might not hear her. Or even if he did, he might have it in his head to keep riding through the weather, just to get back to the hotel. "Ethan!" she called out again.

She was relieved when he turned his bike around and joined her at the bottom of the church steps.

"You take the boys in, and I'll find a place to put the bikes," Izzy said.

Ethan unhitched the trailer from the back of his bike and carried it up the wide steps. The church was as unprepossessing as the town; statues of Mary and Joseph above the entrance served as the sole adornment.

When Izzy entered the church, Ethan was waiting for her in the vestibule, the trailer folded and leaning against a wall. The two boys were tucked under each of his arms. It was cool and dark, the air heavy from the moisture outside. Izzy led Ethan to one of the back pews. Ethan carefully peeled away Tommy's wet rain gear, Izzy did the same for Sam. She saw for the first time that the photographic exteriors ran down the full length of the two figures. Pasted to each boy was a black-and-white image, very lifelike, of overalls. Sam's were rolled up in clean, crisp lines, as were the sleeves of his shirt. Tommy was the less kempt of the two. Izzy wasn't sure what she'd expected. Of course it made sense that there would be clothes under all that outerwear.

"I think they're fine," Izzy said as she inspected Sam for moisture. She now saw that they bent at the hips and knees with Velcro hinges. Ethan was smiling. "Gore-Tex. Best invention ever," he said.

They were so preoccupied with the boys that it took them a minute or two to register what was happening at the front of the church.

"It looks like we've stumbled on choir practice," Izzy said. They settled into the back pew, with the boys on either side of them.

In the back of the apse stood two dozen singers, mostly older adults, here and there a child. A handful of onlookers sat scattered in the front. Rain jackets were slung in decidedly impious fashion across the backs of the pews.

The choir director, a rotund, middle-aged man, said something in Italian that Izzy didn't catch. Whatever it was, it made everyone laugh, especially the younger singers. Once the laughter died down, he paused and then spoke again, this time slowly and deliberately. "Here's another way to think about it: sing as if Mozart were taking dictation directly from God," he said, hitting each word like a nail. As soon as the organ began to play, Izzy recognized the music Mozart had put to the ancient chant, "Ave Verum Corpus."

A fidgety boy standing with the sopranos caught her eye. He was eight or nine and wore a pale-green hoodie and khaki pants at least one size too large. A perpetual motion machine, he took a step forward, and the director quickly turned to him, looking like he was ready to rebuke the boy. Instead, the director raised his right arm, and as he lowered it, the boy's voice rang out in a brief, crystalline solo of two long notes held high and true: "*In mor . . . .*" He possessed an astonishing instrument that reached every cranny of the small church. Izzy had heard this piece many times sung by a full chorus, but never with a solo. And just as it seemed nothing in the world existed outside of that lone incandescent voice, the rest of the choir quietly joined in with underlying harmonies—"*In mor-tis ex-am-ine*"—and the notes descended back to earth, taking with them the boy, whose voice could no longer be heard amid the sea of voices.

Izzy looked at Ethan. She knew how short this chant was. Get distracted for a minute and you've missed it. She wanted to make sure he was hearing it. He sat rapt, a fist held against his mouth.

"*Bello. Bello,*" said the conductor after the final notes tailed off. "*Bellisimo.*"

These few minutes of eternal beauty Izzy and Ethan had just chanced upon caused both of them to turn to look at Tommy and Sam.

"Do you think they heard it?" Ethan asked.

"Yeah," Izzy whispered. "I think so."

"*Grazie, tutti,*" said the conductor. He gave a curlicue wave of his hand, and the group began to disperse. People murmured as they gathered their things and donned their jackets, then nodded and smiled at Ethan and Izzy as they filed past like a wedding recessional.

Only the little boy stopped when he reached their pew. Up close, he looked even smaller, his thick black hair more tousled than it had appeared from afar.

Izzy said something to the boy in Italian. "*Grazie!*" he said, smiling broadly.

Ethan looked at her quizzically.

"I told him he sings beautifully," she said.

The boy was studying Tommy and Sam, and after a moment he shrieked with delight. "What are their names?" he asked in Italian. "Tommy and Sam," Izzy said. "*Ciao,* Tommy and Sam!" the boy said charmingly; then he skipped away.

Izzy looked over at Ethan and noticed an expression on his face that she hadn't seen before—not enraptured, exactly, or confused, or scared, or tormented, but all of these things at once. Izzy was put in mind of the tornado in *The Wizard of Oz*, with chairs and tables swirling around inside the maelstrom.

"Ethan, what is it?" Izzy asked.

Ethan gestured to Tommy and Sam. "You probably wonder why I'm so cautious when it comes to these two," he said.

"I guess, yes, I do," Izzy said.

He was quiet for a minute. The silence between them felt like a pressure on her chest. She looked down at her hands and had a fleeting thought of Gus and their argument. What would he think, seeing them together in this hushed place? It felt almost dangerous. Then Ethan said, "I don't know how to protect people. I didn't protect my parents when I should have."

He was speaking so softly she was having trouble hearing what he said. She inched herself closer to him.

"Protect them?"

"From drowning." He said this matter-of-factly, as if it were something he knew beyond a shadow of a doubt.

Perhaps it was the safety of the church or something about the music, but before she could stop to think, Izzy asked, "Were you with them in the water when it happened?"

"No."

"Where were you?"

Ethan was looking in every direction except Izzy's. "They went on vacation to Hawaii, and I didn't want to go," he said. "It was their first big vacation since I was born. They wanted me to go with them, and I wouldn't go. . . ."

"How old were you?"

"Eight." Now he was bent at the waist, talking to his shoes. It was an unusual position, and she thought immediately of Tommy's and Sam's hinged torsos.

She caught her breath and glanced reflexively at Tommy and Sam. Izzy knew very little about this man, but she did know that whatever she said to him next needed to be thought through carefully. Izzy felt her thigh pressed against Ethan's. Instead of going down through her body, a current of electricity traveled straight to her sternum. This desire to wrap Ethan with her entire body—to hold and protect him, like a mother might—felt all-consuming. She summoned the most innocent question she could think to ask. "Do you remember why you didn't go on the trip?"

She expected him to say no, but instead, he nodded. "It was because of Little League tryouts. I wanted to stay home for them. It was a trip they'd been planning forever; then when the tryouts came up, they couldn't get a refund. So my grandmother came to stay with me for the week."

Ethan's voice was rising and began to fill the church, now empty—the organist, the rumpled conductor, the frisky boy with the angel's voice, and the rest of the choir, all gone.

"My mother had a big brown leather tote bag," Ethan continued. "She carried it everywhere. It was basically her purse. It had short handles so she couldn't even put it over her shoulder. It was totally impractical. It didn't have any side pockets or anything for putting things into, not like the bags you see now. She was always digging around in it, looking for her keys and her wallet and her lipstick."

Ethan had risen to an upright position. "When they were packing for Hawaii, I stuck a couple of Pecan Sandies with a note I wrote into a sandwich bag and snuck it into the leather bag. Now, whenever I think about her, that's what I remember. That scratched-up leather bag and my father teasing her about it."

Izzy waited. Was that all?

"I told her I was sorry," Ethan continued. "I explained that the tryouts really mattered to me and that I'd miss her and I loved her. I wrote a p.s. telling her to be careful when she went into the deep end of the pool. I agonized over how to spell *careful*. I couldn't find the dictionary, so I looked in books and magazines all over the house to find the word. I wanted the note to be perfect."

Ethan's eyes were round, like a child's.

"They were in a pool when they—" Izzy started to ask.

"No," Ethan interrupted, a bit too loudly. Impatience was creeping into his voice. "One of the things they were trying to entice me with was the pool at the hotel, so I knew there would be a pool. I didn't know about the ocean. When the accident happened, I thought she had gone into the deep end of the pool. But she had gone into the ocean and got caught in an undertow. My father went in after her. When their things came back, there was the brown leather bag. The baggie with the Pecan Sandies was still in it, and the cookies were totally crumbled, and the note was there in the middle of the crumbs, all oily from the cookies. I'm pretty sure she never saw it."

Izzy was taking it all in.

"You've never told anyone this, have you?" she asked softly.

Ethan shifted slightly in his seat. He was patting Sam's leg.

She couldn't bear to think that he had been holding it in for all these years. "They were so young," she said.

"Thirty-eight," Ethan said. "They were both thirty-eight."

"Your age?"

He nodded.

"What do you think you could have done to protect them?" Izzy asked.

Now Ethan looked directly at her, taking her by surprise. "I could have been there to stop her." Even in the dim light of the church, Izzy could see a shroud cloaking his eyes. How could a child's grief have contorted so quickly into guilt? She studied the rest of his face for clues. It held a blankness that surely signaled her to pry no further. Still, Sister Genevieve used to tell her students, "Call them in"—with a word or an expression or even a motion of the hand. A voice inside of Izzy urged her to reach deep for even the smallest way she might help bind Ethan Fawcett's wound.

"And you've been carrying this pain all these years?"

"Sometimes I just wake up and I feel . . . I don't know . . . heavy."

"Heavy," she repeated.

Just then, the door to the church opened with a burst of energy and light that made Izzy and Ethan turn their heads. It was the young choir soloist, running down the nave and past their pew. A woman, presumably his mother, stood at the entrance. "Antonio!" she called to him in a loud whisper. "*Piano, Antonio. Non correre!*" Antonio disappeared under a front pew, then popped up a few seconds later and said something to her, shrugging his shoulders, both palms turned up in a theatrical gesture.

Antonio's mother began to follow him, then stopped when she saw Izzy and Ethan. She spoke to them in rapid Italian, offering apologies for disrupting their prayers. Her eyes came to rest on the boys, and just as she seemed to be comprehending the fact that they weren't real, Antonio came galloping toward them, brandishing a small black rolled-up umbrella over his head in triumph. "*Mamma, l'ho trovato!*" He waved at Ethan and Izzy as if he had known them for years. "*Ciao! Ciao*, Tommy! *Ciao*, Sam!"

he called. Then he grinned and added, in English, pronouncing each word with care, "See. You. Later." Pleased with himself, he grabbed his mother's hand and they left the church.

A low sun refracted through prism tiles of stained glass, casting a wide blue light on the opposite wall. The church bell sounded against the silence. Six chimes. People back at the hotel would be getting dressed for dinner. "E-flat," she heard Ethan say, in a voice so low she was sure he didn't intend for her to hear him.

"You know what note that is?" Izzy said.

His brown eyes sparkled, then closed just a smidge longer than a blink. Then he turned to Izzy and smiled.

They emerged from the church into the sunlight to see steam rising from the cobbled pavement. Three women sat on a bench in the small piazza, gossiping and laughing, newspapers spread under them to absorb the water from the rain. Their shopping nets were at their feet, bulging with groceries.

Izzy checked the Garmin. "We're eighteen kilometers from the hotel, so we can get there in forty-five minutes if we ride quickly," she told Ethan.

She took her phone from a pocket of her jacket. There were a dozen text messages from Travis: Had they gotten lost? Had the paper kids wandered off? Been blown away?

By the time they finally cycled up to the hotel entrance, it was nearly dark. Izzy was late for everything: greeting the cyclists with snacks and an end-of-the-day beer, putting the bikes away, the predinner debriefing with the other guides. She had just enough time to change before dinner.

Travis was waiting for her in the lobby. He was clearly pissed.

"Izzy, why weren't you answering my texts?"

"We were in a church."

"A church?" Travis was skeptical. "What were you doing in a church?"

"We had to get out of the rain."

"Of course you did," he said, his voice tinged with sarcasm.

"It's a long story," Izzy said.

Travis let out a long, guttural sigh. "This guy is just more trouble than we can handle."

Oh, how she wished they hadn't been caught in the rain. Then again, if it hadn't rained, they wouldn't have ducked into the church; they wouldn't have come across the choir practice, or Antonio—so exuberant, so full of life—and they wouldn't have heard him sing. If it hadn't rained, Ethan wouldn't have told her about his parents, the baseball tryouts, the grease-stained note. All of this had happened for a reason; she was sure of it. She felt something akin to ecstasy, but tinged with sadness. She knew this was something she couldn't share with Gus. The week with Ethan had made her realize she was changing, growing. This was more than just another bike trip; the week with Ethan had coaxed open an aperture on her life. In helping others, Izzy now realized, she felt herself open to an expanded view of what her own life could be: with Gus, without Gus; working for Hill and Dale, not working for Hill and Dale—so many paths lay ahead. Somehow, Ethan Fawcett had done that for her.

• • • •

The next morning everyone gathered outside with their luggage to take the bus back to Turin. The guides had spent all week hauling suitcases, duffels, and backpacks from hotel to hotel, setting them up inside the rooms, tracking down missing items. Some of the bags had started out light and then, as the week wore on, had grown heavy with bottles of Nebbiolo, Barolo, Moscato.

As the guides helped the driver heave the bags into the belly of his bus, guests who had formed friendships over the course of the week posed for one last set of photos. The Australian family, busy telling others to visit them in Melbourne, looked even more relaxed, even happier than when they had arrived. The Texans were exchanging exuberant hugs with Annette White, trading email addresses and cell numbers, and vowing to stay in touch.

Chauncey and Annette found Izzy while she was on her phone, calling for last-minute restaurant reservations for the Beans, who were staying an extra night in Turin.

"You're a special young woman, Miss Izzy," Chauncey said.

"We hope you'll look us up when you get back to New York," Annette added. "Here's my business card." Izzy's phone buzzed, and up popped the Metropolitan Museum of Art's mod red logo next to her information:

ANNETTE WHITE

SENIOR CURATOR,
DEPARTMENT OF PRINTS AND DRAWINGS

"I like paper," Annette said. Izzy couldn't tell from Annette's tone if she should laugh at the irony, so she just smiled and nodded. She scanned the group for Ethan. Travis had pulled her aside before breakfast to tell her he was recommending a RogerGram for Ethan Fawcett. "I know you like him, Izzy, but he totally disrupted this trip," he'd said. She spotted Ethan apart from the rest of the group. He was carrying Tommy and Sam in their backpack carrier and was busy collapsing the bike trailer. His head was down, his earbuds in.

Izzy gave his shoulder a light tap with one knuckle. He looked up.

"I found something," he said. He removed his earbuds and held his phone up for her to hear. As she listened, he must have seen her bewilderment.

"It's that choir, from the town we stopped in!" he said.

Izzy was peering over at his phone. "'The choir of the Chiesa di San Siro.' They're famous?"

"I'm not sure about that. But they're famous to us. I found this recording online."

Izzy cocked her head slightly as she listened. She couldn't place the music.

"The Mendelssohn *Paulus* oratorio. Pretty ambitious for such a small choir."

"It's beautiful," Izzy said; then she furrowed her brow in concentration. "I'm trying to pick out Antonio."

Ethan took a look at his phone. "This was recorded five years ago. Antonio was probably three."

Izzy laughed. "I have something for you." She handed him the makeshift gift she had put together that morning. "Sorry about the wrapping job," she apologized. The best she could do for wrapping was a paper bag, the fold held down with sports tape.

"Thanks," he said. He showed no apparent interest in unwrapping it. He unzipped his backpack and dropped the package in.

So accustomed was Izzy now to his awkwardness that she took no offense. Anything more would have felt unnatural and stilted.

"Goodbye," Ethan said. His eyes registered gratitude, and maybe a bit of hope—or was Izzy projecting her hope for him? She couldn't tell. Before she could stop to think, Izzy stepped forward and gave Ethan a spontaneous hug. His body stiffened at her touch, and his arms remained at his side. She dropped away; he looked stunned. Then he smiled. "I really enjoyed spending time with you," he said. "You were a great guide." He turned and boarded the bus. She watched him move down the aisle and take a seat, then she saw him bending over to place the boys across the aisle from him. *This is the last image I'll have of him, tending to Tommy and Sam*, she thought. It was breaking her heart to see him come by himself and leave by himself. Where, who, what was he returning to? Did Barb live in Philly too? And did Barb know about Tommy and Sam? Or were they a post-Barb creation?

Then a clamor. Annette was climbing off the bus. "Crap! I forgot my favorite white shirt!" she was saying to no one in particular. "I must have left it on the bed with all those white sheets." She stopped and looked with agitation at the hotel entrance, then shook her head, flustered. "I know it's a total first-world problem hashtag—"

"The hashtag comes first, Hon," Chauncey called through his open window.

"Wait on the bus," Izzy said. "I'll go look for it. I'll be right back."

Five minutes later Izzy was on the bus with the shirt in her hand.

"Angel!" Annette cried out when Izzy handed it to her.

Chauncey started clapping, and everyone else on the bus followed suit. Even grumpy Mr. Bean was clapping. Izzy held out the sides of an invisible skirt and bent one knee in a small curtsey.

She looked up and automatically scanned for Ethan. He was staring out the window, Tommy and Sam straight as soldiers across from him. She saw that Ethan had left their seat belts unbuckled.

Part Three

Ethan

18.

IN RETROSPECT, I SHOULD HAVE SENSED THAT SOMETHING was up when I didn't make dinner for the boys the night Barb came over with the cookies and the letter. That same night, I put them to bed without reading to them first. Truth be told, since returning from the trip, I was skipping their reading on a fairly regular basis.

I had an excuse, and not even a flimsy one. While the boys and I had been away on the bike trip, mice had invaded the house. Usually mice aren't a problem until the cold weather sets in, and it was still August. But the vacant premises must have been irresistible, even though it was plenty warm outside.

Barb and I had battled mice in the past. In an old sieve of a house like ours, the entryways for mice can number in the dozens. And they're relentless. As burrowing animals, mice are designed to squeeze through tight spaces. Their only limiting factor is their skull, one of the few parts of their anatomy made of bone. They don't even have collarbones. Just imagine all the holes you could squeeze through if you didn't have a clavicle. Mice flatten themselves to credit-card thickness, and before you know it, there they are, up through your floorboards and into your box of shredded wheat.

Mice are also excellent climbers. They have little trouble free-soloing vertical walls and finding wires that extend to the roofline.

But we kept them at bay, thanks to a combination of constant vigilance, food in airtight containers, and linens stored in a tin-lined closet (we dubbed it the mouse closet) that had survived from the original house. But while I was in Italy, they'd crawled up from the basement and in through the floorboards. They'd entered via closets and the back door. They'd dropped down from the attic into the bedrooms.

They made hay all over the place, but the pantry, where I'd forgotten to seal all of the food in hard plastic containers, was hit like a cyclone. The mice must have arrived shortly after we left, because by the time we got home, the little walk-in pantry was peppered with hundreds of mouse droppings, on the floor, on the shelves, on top of boxes.

I triaged the pantry situation according to severity. I threw out everything that wasn't in a jar or can. It took me days to clean up the mess.

Upstairs, the mice had helped themselves to the bedding. Even the soap was chewed on. Who knew that mice liked to eat soap?

Rooting out the critters took weeks. I set miniature Havahart traps. I couldn't bear to kill them, especially now that they were fattened and healthy and happy with life, having feasted on our food for more than a week. Better to give the jolly mice a chance to do good in the world.

Every morning, I released my overnight catch of two or three, sometimes more, into Mike the Cat's pet carrier, took the bus to the Penn campus, and delivered them to Lena and Dirk—a couple of psych researchers, and friends of Barb's, as it happened—who were studying anxiety. They were skeptical. Laboratory mice, they told me, had to be free of pathogens and were strictly regulated. Wild mice such as mine (I couldn't exactly claim these mice as "mine," but I didn't press the point) would have to go through a period of quarantine. Even then, they couldn't guarantee they'd be able to use them in their research. But they took the mice anyway.

In the thick of the mouse invasion, I found myself taking less time to prepare full meals for the boys, instead cobbling together a series of snacks. My own meals traveled straight from the freezer to the microwave. The purging of the house, the setting of the traps, and the daily trips to Penn and back were all-consuming. In the middle of this, a physical version of the Hill and Dale letter disinviting me from future trips arrived in the mail. It was caught in the folds of a Bed Bath & Beyond flyer; the thin envelope fluttered to the ground when I was outside chucking junk mail into the recycling bin. I stacked it with other mail, unopened, and forgot about it.

The boys' lessons, too, went by the wayside. Sometimes I caught a glimpse of the whiteboard, unchanged since before the bike trip. Brushing against it as I vacuumed my way across the living room one afternoon, my T-shirt (which could easily have been mistaken for a rag anyway) rubbed away some of the world capitals: we lost Lima, Santiago, Brasília, and part of Buenos Aires. It occurred to me to resurrect those cities for the sake of educational completeness, but I didn't. That same afternoon, when I was moving the credenza where the TV sat to replace a trap, the power strip popped out of the wall, and the *Columbo* episode the boys were watching went dead. I left the strip on the floor. I should have felt guilty; instead, I was indifferent.

As long as I'm in a confessional frame of mind, I'll go ahead and tell you the worst thing I did, the act that set into motion the entire series of events for the next few days.

The weather was lovely those days, and once the house was clean, I went into our small backyard to do some yard work. I'd never been much of a gardening type—this was another task that had tended to fall into Barb's column—but now it seemed right to take out the shears and the rake to tidy things up. I liked the way our little garden looked when I was done. As the sun set on my second day of gardening, with what looked like rain clouds beginning to roll in, I finally, two days later, plugged the TV back in and sat down on the couch next to the boys. Tommy, possessing the dominant personality, insisted on *Sesame Street*. Sam wanted to switch to *Mister Rogers*. I was quietly rooting for Sam, who was wearing his Fred Rogers cardigan. I was proud of him for stating his preference, for finally speaking up. I thought I'd let the two of them work it out. But I felt hollow and carved out and didn't really care to watch television at all. The room was silent, though Tommy and Sam had just been arguing about which show to watch. I strained to hear their voices. And yet . . . nothing. They sat on the couch in silence, staring straight ahead.

"Enough with the squabbling, you two!" I said sharply. I took both boys, hitched them under my arm, carried them outside, and put them in the patio chairs, in nothing but their overalls (though Sam also had on his cardigan). I stood for a moment, trying to calm myself, taking in the garden, the anemones in full, tall, glorious bloom. They looked so animated and alive. I glanced at the boys, who sat inert. I stalked back into the house, locked the sliding door behind me with an unambiguous click, went upstairs, and climbed into bed.

An hour or so later, still awake, I heard the sound of rain outside. As it picked up, I felt awful . . . but also strangely exhilarated. I lay in bed for a good twenty minutes listening to the drops hit the bedroom windows. Then I got up. "This is insane," I said out loud. I bolted down the stairs and brought the boys inside. I carried them upstairs to the bathroom and put them in the tub. A soggy smell filled the room. I found the space heater and plugged it in. Then I went all over the house in a frantic search for my phone. I finally found it in the kitchen. It was 10:48 p.m. I called Barb.

She answered on the second ring. I tried to talk but couldn't say a thing.

"Ethan, are you okay?"

"I'm not sure," I finally replied. I started to explain what had happened—the gardening, *Sesame Street*, the time-out, and, finally, the rain.

"I'm coming over," she said.

She was at the house inside of ten minutes. She was wearing an old pair of sweatpants with pockets, her favorite baggy sweater, and her scuffed-up clogs. She had a tote bag from a psychology conference—APS/2016—slung over her shoulder. She looked beautiful.

Barb knew just what to do. She pulled two towels off the rack, laid them on the bathroom floor, gingerly lifted the boys from the tub, and placed them on the towels. Then she pulled a small foldable hair dryer out of her tote bag. But the bathroom, being so old, didn't have an outlet. She knew just where to find an extension cord—in her old office, under the desk. I heard her clattering around in the room before she returned with the longer cord.

She waved the blow-dryer up and down and back and forth, first on Sam, then on Tommy. The thing was loud and it made conversation impossible. It sucked so much wattage that the lights flickered. Her hand hovered over the spots where the rain had really drenched the boys. I was so grateful to her. Not only had I never used a blow-dryer, but I had never seen Barb use one. Nonetheless, she wielded it as if born with the device in her hand.

When she turned the dryer off, the quiet was eerie. Sam's upper torso had been protected by the sweater, but his face was ripped in a jagged line down one side of his left cheek, like a dueling scar. The edge of Tommy's overalls was peeling away.

"Oh, Ethan, I'm so sorry," Barb said, her expression tender, displaying no trace of the annoying condescension from a few weeks earlier, when she'd shown up with the cookies and the Hill and Dale letter.

We settled ourselves down on the bathroom floor like a couple of kindergartners. The boys sat up against one wall, and we were leaning against the tub, facing them.

To her great credit, Barb didn't ask me why I had done it.

"It's all going to be okay," she said, her mother's cheekbones rising on her face. Since she'd left, Barb had started looking more and more like Bunny.

"I know you wanted the best for us . . . and our family," I said.

"Yes, I did."

"Then I lost myself."

"We all do at times. But if I'd known how vulnerable you were, I never would've brought them home. I opened a door I never should have opened—but I didn't even know what was behind it. And you walked straight through it."

"You opened so many other doors for me. I couldn't . . . ." I was nearly choking with grief. My speech sounded to me like the rapid clicking sound a car makes when the starter dies.

"I'm not sure how to put this," she said, running her hand over the tufted bath mat on the floor between us. "It might seem to you like you did something terrible, but you know this is a good thing?" I read her statement-slash-question as an exhortation. "Do you think that leaving the boys in the rain might have been about something else?"

I must have looked confused because she went on. "We gave the boys great personalities. It felt good in the beginning. It felt like something private and meaningful."

Now she lifted that same hand that had been smoothing the mat and placed it over mine. "I mean, lately I started wondering who the real boys in the photographs were," she said. "Who they were on their own terms. So I did some research." She was gazing straight ahead, and so was I. We were two people in a car, staring out at the road ahead of us.

"I found the photo on the Library of Congress website. I told you their names were Tommy and Sam, but I made those names up. In the photo, they're just described as two young farm boys."

"How did you even know where to look?" I asked.

"I had a hunch it was a Dorothea Lange photo."

"Who?"

"Dorothea Lange," she said.

I confessed that I didn't know who she was.

"She was an amazing photographer who traveled all over the country with her camera documenting life in rural America during the Depression. The photo of the two boys is part of a group of photos she took in North Carolina in 1939, in a place called Person County. The boys were probably the kids of sharecroppers. A lot of the people she photographed are just labeled 'white sharecropper,' or 'wife of sharecropper,' or 'Negro tenant.' Just think about the lives those two boys had, growing up white and poor in the Jim Crow South, not even eighty years after the Civil War. And that troublemaker we named Tommy . . . ." We both looked at Tommy, his sly grin speaking volumes. "Well, I decided it might be best *not* to know what he might have done with his life. And the fact is, we don't know and never will. Those boys most likely grew into men who would have both died by now."

She rummaged in her tote bag and pulled out her phone. "Here," she said. "Here's the photo." She held her phone out to me. There were our two scrawny boys, in one black-and-white photograph, standing barefoot on parched, dusty earth. I recognized it as a nitrate negative, with the identification "20124-E" written backward across the top.

"They look . . . ," I began.

"Destitute," Barb said, finishing my thought. She had pulled one knee to her chest and had the phone balanced on it. Our heads were canted toward each other as we looked at the photo. "And maybe not even that aware of how destitute they are."

"Yeah," I said. "Not unhappy."

"Not unhappy," she echoed. Her phone screen went dark and she put the phone back in her bag. "The point is that the boys had their own story. It's a story we weren't part of." She was quiet for a moment, then said, "That's true about your parents too."

I felt as if she were blowing each word toward me through a bubble wand, their shifting shapes buoyed by the warm air. "I'm just wondering," she said. She paused, then continued, "I'm just wondering if there might be a more helpful way of understanding that tragedy."

I heard myself take in a quick breath. My parents. Two people who loved each other well before I was born, who died together. One trying to save the other. I had no part in that story. Barb had known this all along.

The musty, humid smell in the bathroom had mingled with Barb's sweet lavender scent. Now her eyes were on me; they held a softness I hadn't seen since well before she'd moved out. Floating loosely somewhere in my mind was an image of the people we once were, not so long ago.

"In Italy . . . ," she paused. I waited. "Did you go to the monastery?"

"Yes," I said. "It was still beautiful, but it felt like just another hotel."

"Was the chess set still there?"

I flashed on our game of chess at that hotel. "I don't remember," I said. I couldn't recall the chess set, but now that she'd mentioned it, the stay at the monastery with Barb came back to me in granular detail. In fact, when I had been there the second time, I could think of nothing else: our retreat to our room on the day of the bicycle fiasco; the delicious afternoon lunch; our speculation on who might have cut the bike cables.

I said none of that to Barb. Just this: "And this time the guides locked the bikes away inside."

We laughed.

Then we grew quiet. And before I was even aware I was speaking, I said this: "I think I might have a plan for the boys."

"Really?" She was clearly curious.

"I'm still trying to figure it out."

She stood up. The blow-dryer made a declarative plastic-on-plastic sound as Barb snapped it back together. Then she wound the cord around the appliance and stuffed it into her tote bag. She was looking at her big wristwatch. "I should get going. It's past midnight. Are you going to be okay? Will you get some help?"

"I will." With that *I will*, I meant, *I can*. It was an *I will* entirely different from the *I will* I had voiced in front of all those wedding guests at the Mütter Museum, when Frank had asked about my willingness to care for Barb, to meet her needs, to tend to her heart. Yes, my willingness then had known no bounds. But *was* I now able? She didn't ask. For then, as now, I'd have said, "I don't think so." Or perhaps, "But look at me. Look at what I have to work with." Barb had tried her utmost. I didn't know where or how to begin. Those were the stark, unadorned facts of the case. The evidence wasn't circumstantial. I was my own smoking gun. And yet this time I felt a twinge of hope. I had bared myself to Izzy, who had made me feel so safe, and now perhaps the avuncular therapist, Dr. Schatz, or some other expert, could help me.

"Ethan," Barb suddenly said. "You're thirty-eight!"

"I am," I said.

"How was your birthday?"

"It was good," I replied. "There was cake. And someone on the trip wrote me a poem."

After Barb left, I stayed in the bathroom with the boys for a long while. Finally, I left them on the tiled floor with the space heater turned on low and wandered back to bed. I slept fitfully. I dreamed about the choir rehearsal, the one Izzy and I had stumbled upon in Italy. My dreaming mind transported the whole choir from the inside of the church to the outside, to the patch of brown dirt from the photo Barb had shown me. Tommy and Sam were there, too, in the soprano section, standing next to Antonio, that little boy with the angel's voice. But Antonio made my boys look as tiny as thimbles, dwarfed by the sheer existence of this real child. Tommy and Sam both had their mouths open in perfect round O's. But they made no sound.

· · · ·

The next morning when I poured half-and-half into my coffee and watched it swirl down into the brown-black brew, I thought of Barb's words from the night before. *Vulnerable* is what she'd called me. And she blamed herself for underestimating the depth of my fear of parenting.

Now I'd had a full night to digest all that she'd told me. She said that one afternoon while I'd been away at an off-site meeting, she'd spent the afternoon working in the library at the Mütter Museum. As she was leaving for the day, she'd noticed that the museum was in the process of dismantling an exhibit about health scourges during the Great Depression. She saw the boys, one photo divided into two life-size figures constructed of sturdy corrugated cardboard.

She said they looked so dejected and at the same time their faces so full of life, their personalities so distinct, that she'd stopped to admire them. A museum staffer told her they were headed for the recycling bin, and Barb asked if she could take them. She carried them home on the bus, put them on the couch, and waited for me to return.

At first, she said, she thought they'd be a fun little prop. But just before I got home, she decided to pretend they were real boys. She led me into the living room to introduce me to our so-called foster children, named Tommy and Sam and taken in as a favor to Frank. She had made up their names on the spot, along with the whole Frank part, of course. It was part of the joke. But her acquisition of the boys wasn't entirely a joke. Aware of my parental ambivalence, she was high on the idea of practicing at having kids, much the way newly married couples try their hand at a pet dog before having children.

I tried to conjure some of the details from the moment I met the boys, but my memory was locked. I recalled only the haziest outlines. I remembered that something had told me to resist this game. But Barb had made it all seem so harmless. And it was. Or should have been. Before long, I was all in. I was the one who'd conferred personalities on the boys and, most of all, a keen need for protection. When Barb tried to get through to me, first by telling me I was in danger of slipping away, then by putting me on high alert, I'd paid no heed.

. . . .

The rain continued throughout the day, and since I was stuck inside, I decided to declutter the house for the first time in months. I could suddenly see that the place was a mess. I hadn't even bothered to unpack in the weeks since the trip, or to do laundry. I had tossed my backpack, hypoallergenic snacks and all, into a corner of the living room. The boys were on the couch, but the TV was off. I dreaded looking at them, given their condition. And mine.

As I emptied out the backpack, I found the package Izzy had given me on the last morning of the trip. It was wrapped in a brown paper bag, taped shut. Inside was a small tin of Melighe cookies. There was a note with it: "Ethan, I'm so glad our paths crossed. Let me know if you're ever in New York. xo, Izzy." She had added her cell number.

I opened the tin and plucked out a cookie. It was crumbly and not too sweet. She must have remembered that during the trip I had dubbed it the perfect cookie. Izzy was a true friend. I got my phone and texted her: "Hi Izzy. It's Ethan Fawcett. Are you back in New York? I'm thinking of coming up there."

Actually, I hadn't been thinking of going to New York until that moment. But now, if she said yes, there was no turning back.

She responded at once: "Hi Ethan! Of course! I'm back in New York. Just let me know when."

We made a date for that Friday, in two days' time.

As I was putting the phone down, I saw a new text from her: "It will be great to see you."

That was just like Izzy, going out of her way to say something nice even after a conversation had ended.

19.

THE MORNING OF THE TRIP, I HINGED THE BOYS AT THE waist and knees and folded each third, so they made a compact bundle. I put them in a large duffel bag, which I zipped, but not all the way. Sheer force of habit.

I arrived at 30th Street Station a good half hour early. The pandemic had mostly receded, but a recent uptick in cases had led to masks once again being required on public transit. I cinched my mask under my glasses, boarded the train within a minute of the posting of the track, and got a row to myself. I put the duffel on the seat next to me. I had my earbuds in (Bobby McFerrin doing Bach), but I could still hear passengers enter behind me; I watched the backs of their heads as they continued down the aisle, the threat dissolving as each one shuffled past, then rising again when another one approached. A psychological Doppler effect.

When I got off at Penn Station in New York and climbed the stairs, I couldn't believe how crowded it was with people who still somehow managed to give each other a wide berth.

My phone buzzed. A text from Izzy: "I'm here under the clock."

I spotted her instantly. She was wearing a black denim jacket, jeans, and desert boots. It occurred to me that I had only seen her out of biking gear a handful of times. She was a good five foot six but looked more diminutive—though not at all diminished—in regular clothes. She was staring down at her phone but looked up as soon as I was within fifty feet of her, as if she had an extra eye on the side of her head. She waved. A faint line of puzzlement ran across her forehead, which I assumed was because she didn't see the carrier on my back.

She gave me a hug, which felt a little strange. In Italy we were a pod, but a hug here, in the US, after weeks apart, seemed just a bit reckless. Oddly, I didn't mind.

I thought New York would make Izzy different—a more clipped person, maybe, or brusque. But she was as mellow and genial as ever—which seemed even more extraordinary amid the frenzy, like seeing Gandhi in the stands at an NFL game.

"How was the train?" she asked as we rode the escalator up to Seventh Avenue.

"Easy," I said.

I thought I might ask her a question—I wasn't sure what—when she launched straight into the lunch plan. She'd chosen a ramen restaurant a few blocks south on Seventh Avenue, in the same direction the cars and yellow cabs were barreling. I know there are people who love New York City, but I've never been among them. And now, the number of people on the sidewalks maintaining a constant distance from one another, like magnets with like poles, was a guaranteed nerve jangler. Add to that the number of people walking around with their eyes locked on their phones. My neck hurt just looking at them. Still, as Izzy and I walked along, I felt a sense of well-being I couldn't quite account for. New York felt different because I felt different. From the minute I'd gotten off the train, even before seeing Izzy, I'd felt a springiness beneath me, and now it was as if the sidewalk had a trampoline bounce to it.

The restaurant was clean and spare, with dimmable recessed ceiling lights. A narrow central aisle was flanked by what looked like office cubicles on either side, each separated by high dividers. "They're called flavor-concentration booths," Izzy explained, though it didn't sound like an explanation of anything. "It's a solo-dining restaurant." She told me they could accommodate the two of us. Each of the dining booths was named after a place in Japan—Konose, Ichinomori, Tsurugi, Ino—and for those waiting in line for a table, the booth would light up and buzz when it was ready. The diner would then head off to slurp noodles in culinary solitary confinement. This chain of ramen restaurants had been a couple of years ahead of the pandemic, not with health as a top priority, Izzy told me, but with the optimization of taste buds in mind. The idea, Izzy said, is that ramen deserves one's full attention and should be experienced without distraction. Solo ramen eating had taken off years earlier in Japan, and now the divider concept had come to restaurants all over the place. Izzy told me that she and her boyfriend (Gus—she'd told me about Gus, another Hill and Dale guide) were big ramen fans, and this was one of their favorites.

In a concession to parties of more than one, the dividers between cubicles were removable. Standing there waiting for our table, looking down at the solo diners waiting in line in front of us, I understood the principle, but each divider seemed like a monument to isolation, a codification of loneliness. I looked back on my life of relative isolation, all those lonely meals at Miss Flo's Diner before meeting Barb. After she'd come along, whenever we ate a meal together, food actually tasted far better than it ever did when I ate alone. Maybe my mouth was somehow connected to my psyche, both awakened, or deadened, in sync. I wondered if this might be a topic Barb could explore in her research.

Whatever the solo experience took away from profit margins of bigger groups at the same table, the restaurant made up for it with quick turnaround from no conversation. Before long two adjacent booths lit up. Izzy was in Nagoro. I was next to her in Ochi. We folded the divider back and there we sat in our neat row on round stools with red padded seats. At the back of the cubicles was a screen that looked like a vertical tatami mat.

Instead of placing an order with a human, you filled out a form; then with the push of a button you summoned your server to retrieve it—all without words exchanged. "It's all about zero interaction," Izzy said without a hint of judgment. When people refrain from judgment, I usually question their intelligence. But in the case of Izzy (she's plenty smart), it was a signature feature of the way she lived her life, with an empathetic rather than a critical eye.

Despite its emphasis on solitude, the restaurant was noisy, with a lot of bells and other dinging. The call button for the server made a loud electronic chime. And people were talking on their phones, so there was no need to feel self-conscious about having a conversation.

THE BOYS

We filled out our order forms (our server had written her name on the forms: Alicia). We then pressed the button, and the tatami mat screen rose mysteriously. Alicia arrived to pick up the order slips. We saw only a slice of her—from her chest to the top of her thighs, like a badly cropped photo. She was wearing an orange T-shirt and an orange, green, and black apron.

A few minutes later, the tatami screen lifted and a pair of pale female hands placed bowls of broth and noodles in front of each of us. The steam from my bowl rose with the steam from Izzy's in a harmonic whorl. Alicia turned to the side, placed her hands together, and bowed, giving us an ever-so-brief glimpse of her face; then she lowered the screen.

As we waited for our broth to cool, Izzy asked the inevitable. "How are Tommy and Sam?"

"I brought them," I said, and I nodded at the duffel in a gesture not unlike the bow from our ramen waitress.

Izzy looked down, then back up at me. She seemed confused.

I bent over, picked up the duffel, put it on my lap, and unzipped it.

There they were—Tommy's sweet unchanging face was jammed up against the side of the bag, and Sam was scrunched next to him, half his face ripped. It was an excruciating unveiling, like the coroner unzipping a body bag in the morgue to show the next of kin.

Izzy looked horrified. "What happened? Did they get wet?"

I told her about the series of small acts of neglect after the bike trip, starting with the night I decided not to make them dinner. Every day became a drama of inattention, I told her, leading up to that one radical act when I'd left them in the rain. I wasn't looking at Izzy, but I could tell she was nodding.

"I . . . they . . . ." I was trying to get to the point. *Watch yourself, Ethan*, I said silently. Where to go from here? I did everything except say the words I needed to say. I felt a planet away from the contents of that duffel, almost as if I had no clue what was in there.

My idea had started out loose and unformed in my mind; then each time I circled around to it, it had taken on more definition. I finally cut to the chase. "Are you going back to Italy?" We were both slurping our ramen.

"I'm going in a few weeks," she said. "A couple of us are going to ride some of the routes to start planning for next summer."

"Do you remember the village in Italy with all the cloth people?"

"How could I forget?" she said.

"I was thinking Tommy and Sam might like to go—" I caught myself. "I think they'd fit in well."

Her face brightened. "With Signora Fiore!"

My broth slurped, the noodles sucked, the pork discs and chopped scallions chewed and swallowed, I now had both hands in the pockets of my fleece jacket.

The boys were lying across both our laps, Tommy's head on Izzy's knees, Sam's on mine. What a sight we must have presented to all those hipster ramen eaters. I prayed we wouldn't end up on someone's Instagram feed.

I'm not sure how long we sat there. Izzy would take an afternoon and drive the Hill and Dale van to the village. She remembered exactly where it was. She would find the lady with the wagon and ask her to look after the boys. She would suggest they join the sister's class in the school.

"I like your idea a lot, Ethan," she said quietly. "Do you want to say goodbye?"

"I already have," I told her. My throat got a knotted feeling that extended halfway down my chest. But it all made sense. I had given Tommy and Sam personalities, but just as the cloth people represented people who had once lived, that photograph of two unnamed boys in the Depression-era South was a photograph of people who had been real. The photos themselves, I knew, were not.

We took our time walking back up Seventh Avenue, then over to Eighth, taking wide arcing detours around our fellow pedestrians. After a few more blocks north, Izzy turned to me and said, "This is where I peel off for the subway." I held the duffel bag out to her and she took it, then slowly set it down on the ground at her feet. "I'm really glad you came to New York," she said.

I was looking down at the duffel, picturing the boys stowed in an overhead bin on a plane. I winced. "They can't go in the . . . ," I began. An ambulance was screaming down Seventh Avenue, drowning out my words. I let it drop.

"I couldn't hear you," she said after the ambulance passed.

"I was just saying . . . thank you."

She stepped forward and put her arms around me. Instead of stiffening, this time I gave as good as I got, relaxing into this gift without words. I held on for an extra second or two, surprising us both. The duffel was between us and we were leaning over it, forming a perfect arch. After the hug, Izzy held on to my shoulders and looked me straight in the eye. "You are so much more amazing than you can possibly know," she said. She bent over and picked up the bag, then turned and walked east, the duffel bumping softly against her side. As I watched her disappear down the block, she seemed almost a mystical figure, briefly my gift alone, but now, absorbed into the crowd, everyone's.

From where I stood, Penn Station was a few hundred yards. I retraced the route we'd taken on our way to lunch, turning left on Thirty-First Street. I found myself walking behind a man with a ponytail wearing a Captain America shield backpack and a bowler hat. I trailed him for that one long block and found myself wondering where he was headed and who would have a Captain America shield backpack. When I reached the corner of Eighth Avenue and Thirty-First Street, Captain America walked on while I stopped to admire the columns and Corinthian capitals of the imposing General Post Office building, along with its pronouncement that neither snow nor rain nor heat nor gloom of night would deter brave couriers from delivering Bed Bath & Beyond coupons. And please-go-away letters from Hill and Dale Adventures. But even the reminder of that letter didn't bother me so much.

Penn Station, I now saw, had been transformed from the dark and miserable train hub I had always known it to be. Had I not even noticed this when I'd arrived a few hours earlier? The entrance to the new Moynihan Train Hall had a welcoming appeal to it; natural light poured in through the soaring glass ceiling. According to the cube-shaped clock that hung from the center of the gleaming concourse, it was 2:50 p.m. A line was forming to descend the escalator for Track 11 and the 3:00 p.m. Acela bound for Washington. With everyone headed out of town for the weekend, the train back to Philly was crowded but quiet, an oasis compared to the goings-on in the streets of Midtown above. I found a row with two empty seats and settled in next to the window. Just when it looked like the coast was clear and I'd have the row to myself, along came a woman (my age? slightly older? slightly younger?). "Are you okay with my sitting here?" she asked. "No problem," I said. She had long straight brown hair and a fringe of bangs that brushed the tops of her eyebrows. She was wearing glasses with large black frames, a black peacoat over a plaid skirt, and black tights. As soon as she sat down, she took her Kindle out of her bag and started reading. With all the Kindles and iPads these days, there's no more peeking at dust jackets; we've lost the ability to assess total strangers according to the books in their hands. How are you supposed to judge a book by its cover if it doesn't have one?

I pulled that morning's *Philadelphia Inquirer* from my backpack and scanned the headlines. But I kept sneaking a peek at my seatmate's ebook. From the way she had it tilted, I couldn't see a single word. I felt a pressing need to know what the book was. I wanted to ask, but without Barb, my question-asking muscle had atrophied. My heart began to pound. A shot of adrenaline landed in my fingertips. Before I could test word choice and intonation in my head, the question tumbled out of my mouth, filling the narrow shaft of air that separated us.

"So what are you reading?" To my own ear my voice sounded much too loud and a half step too high.

She looked up. "Total escapist junk," she said. She caught my gaze. "I'm Lisa," she said.

"Nice to meet you, Lisa," I replied, completely forgetting to offer my name in return. "You weren't named after a computer by any chance, were you?" I asked, on a hunch.

"Yes, I was!" she said. She told me she was born in 1983, the year the Lisa computer was introduced. Her parents had met while working at Apple.

"Good thing you weren't born in 1984," I said. Scarcely missing a beat, she laughed, a delicate chuckle in a merry one-two of

F and A in quick succession. "You're right. My name would be Macintosh!" Our eyes met for a moment, but I was spent. She turned back to her ebook.

The odd part is that this woman, Lisa, didn't resemble Barb one bit, but it was Barb who came to my mind's eye, Barb for whom I felt a sudden longing. A slender crescent of hope rose unbidden and rocked gently in my chest.

The train began moving slowly out of the station and through the dark tunnel under the Hudson. I felt New York receding and the boys and Izzy somewhere back there too. We began to pick up speed, and soon we were whizzing along, the last slants of lemon-colored light strobing in through the grimy window. It should have been a blur, but everything was in perfect focus: trees and bushes and people's backyards, filled with rusted swing sets, old cars, an above-ground swimming pool, a pile of old tires. The images of this quick-moving zoetrope passed before me against the still, azure sky.

My phone pulsed from inside my pocket.

It was a text from Barb: "How are you?"

I responded at once: "I'm good. The plan for the boys is underway."

No sooner had I sent it than up popped the pulsing dot-dot-dot bubble, followed by just this:

My thumbs flew: "What's the first song on the jukebox at Miss Flo's?"

"A1 = Elvis. Can't Help Falling . . ."

"If we started at 7 tonight we'd make it through the list by midnight."

"See you there at 7," she wrote back. A pause, then more dots. "Let's take it a song at a time."

Acknowledgments

Many kind, patient, generous souls helped get this flight of imagination off the ground. For their wise counsel, thanks to: Beate Becker, Tony Bianco, Marjorie Campbell, Mary Cappello, Kirsten Colantino, Julie Crutcher, Greg Dreicer, Jim and Deb Fallows, Sarah Glazer, Sarah Greene, Bunny Healy, Fred Khedouri, Ken Krushel, Amy-Jill Levine, Judy Lin, Amy and Howard Neukrug, Paul Schorin, Matt Segall, Alda Sigmundsdóttir, Deborah Unger, Sr. M. Gervaise Valpey, and Elizabeth Younan. For helpful reads of early drafts: Jessica Fechtor, Alison Gwinn, Cristela Henriquez, Mollie Katzen, Marissa Moss, Lee Pollack, Jessica Raimi, Sherry Turkle, and Meredith White. For Italian lessons: Karen Antonelli and Antoinette and Antonio Valla. For a place to perch: Lucy and Carmelo Boas, Nancy Boas, Patricia Larsen, Susan and Larry Levy, Dean Schillinger and Ariella Hyman, and Cathie and Chris Warner.

Every possible permutation of "thank you" goes to my Writing Girls, Sue Scott and Allison Thomas, and to Debra Jo Immergut for her artful edit of a late draft. I got lucky when Barrett Briske stepped in with her sharp copyediting and Rachel Kowal with her sharp proofreading. For their publishing savvy, thanks to Nicole Dewey, Julie Grau, Amy Metsch, Courtney Paganelli, and Liza Wachter. Jim Levine couldn't have been a more ardent advocate. My eternal thanks to Cindy Spiegel for knowing what this book was about before I did.

Bob Wachter has my infinite love and gratitude, as together we increasingly resemble our dog. And Zoë Lyon, thank you for saying these four words back in 2017 after hearing the tiniest tidbit of a story: "Mom, *that's* a novel."

Reading Group Guide

1. Katie Hafner said in an interview that one of her goals in writing *The Boys* was to create a novel in which all the characters are, at their core, good people. Why might an author set a goal like this one—and what do you think of such a goal for a novel? Do you believe she succeeded? Can you think of other novels in which all the characters, despite their flaws or missteps, are people who consistently try to do the right thing?

2. Ethan describes himself as socially awkward and taciturn, with his quiet introversion a stark contrast to Barb's outgoing nature. Their pairing in *The Boys* might be seen as a case of "opposites attract." Does this adage ring true to you? Was their relationship convincing to you, or could you see the end in sight? Are you more drawn to people with whom you share qualities or those who are radically different?

3. One of Ethan's professional talents lies in reverse engineering. As he describes it, "It's like being given a slice of cake, then being told to unbake it and produce the recipe and list the raw ingredients." How might the narrative structure of *The Boys* serve as an example of reverse engineering? How would you understand this story differently if it had been told in a conventional, chronological way—beginning with Ethan meeting Barb? What can doing things in reverse reveal that a linear approach might not?

4. When you first recognized the surprising twist of the novel, what was your reaction? Did you see it coming, or was it completely unexpected? Did it deepen the themes of the novel for you, and if so, in what ways? Did you feel Hafner's narrative decision was a feat of storytelling or did you feel annoyed that she withheld crucial information? Can you think of other books or films that contain a twist or surprise that made you reevaluate the entire work?

5. From automated phone calls to the social isolation of the pandemic and even Ethan's self-imposed solitude, emotional distance and disconnect permeate *The Boys*. In her research, Barb makes the "clear distinction between social isolation and loneliness," claiming that "it's possible to be socially isolated without feeling lonely." Discuss the themes of loneliness and solitude in the book.

6. Given the isolation so many felt during Covid, do you consider this novel a pandemic novel or one simply set during a pandemic? To what extent do you think the pandemic is a trigger for the breakdown of Ethan and Barb's relationship? Would their conflict have occurred regardless of the pandemic? How might things have played out differently in other circumstances? One

result of the pandemic is the intensification of Ethan's peculiarities and personality tics, for example, his reclusiveness and his fears of the outside world. Which of your behaviors were magnified during the pandemic? How might your habits have changed for better or for worse?

7. Midway through the Italy bike trip, Gus, Izzy's boyfriend, asks her, "What do you think makes Ethan tick?" Izzy struggles to give a complete answer but says she is taken by "something so pure about him and his love for the boys." Do you agree with her assessment? How would you answer Gus's question? When in the novel did you feel you understood Ethan the best? And conversely, at which points did his thoughts or actions seem incomprehensible?

8. Ethan finds an unlikely kinship with Signora Fiore, the elderly Italian woman distributing cloth people around her deserted village to replace those who have left or passed away. Like Ethan, Signora Fiore "imbue[s] non-people with people-like traits," projecting her own world onto what is no longer there. What are the similarities and differences between the cloth people and Tommy and Sam? Signora Fiore's ritual of placing the cloth people around the village appears to be a way for her to grieve and memorialize her community. Where would you draw the line between an unreality that is cathartic and one that is delusional?

9. When we return to Ethan's perspective, we learn that he is somewhat aware that the boys began as a shared fiction between him and Barb. He says: "Barb had made it all seem so harmless. And it was. Or should have been. Before long, I was all in. I was the

one who conferred personalities on the boys, and most of all, a keen need for protection." Yet Ethan also says that he cannot fully remember the moment when he met them, recalling only the "haziest outlines." How aware do you think Ethan is that the boys are not real?

10. Through Barb, we learn that Tommy and Sam originate from a photograph taken by Dorothea Lange during the Great Depression and that their reality is far removed from the backstories given to them. Why is this revelation significant? What do you know about this period in history, and do you want to know more about the real lives of these boys? How would you feel if your own image was repurposed in this way?

11. The novel closes with Ethan reconciling with Barb, returning to Miss Flo's, the jukebox, and the early rituals of their relationship, though there is still a lot of work to do to heal the breach between them. Do you feel optimistic about their future together? What has changed and what needs to happen next to repair their marriage?

About the Author

Katie Hafner is a journalist and author who writes frequently for the *New York Times* and the *Washington Post*. She is the author of six non-fiction books, including the memoir *Mother Daughter Me, A Romance on Three Legs: Glenn Gould's Obsessive Quest for the Perfect Piano, The House at the Bridge: A Story of Modern Germany*, and *Where Wizards Stay Up Late: The Origins of the Internet* (with Matthew Lyon). She is host and co-executive producer of the podcasts *Lost Women of Science* and *Our Mothers Ourselves*. *The Boys* is her first novel. She lives in San Francisco with her husband, Bob Wachter, and their dog, Newman.